Book 1 in The Dark Angel Trilogy

The Dark Angel Trilogy is a work of fiction. Names, characters, places and incidents are the products of the author's imagination. Any resemblance to actual persons, living or dead, events, or locales is entirely coincidental.

This book is dedicated to my family and friends, who supported me and stood by me while I struggled and fought with the entire process.

A special thanks to my best friend Pam Scholl Rockcastle, who stepped up to edit the book when I thought I was never going to find someone and to my Dad who read, critiqued and gave me advice on the book. I love you both!

Prologue

My name is Aingeal Ó Cuinn, and I am twenty three years old. I am a high school graduate majoring in art with a minor in English and I've always wanted to go to that great art college in Manhattan but never had time since I have to work for a living. I've dreamed of traveling and being free all my life, but I am stuck here until I can find my big break.

I never really had an exciting life; spent more time in my art studio than with my friends as a kid. Now during the nights you can usually find me working in a local tavern; waiting customers, cleaning tables, and the usual dealings associated with that job. During the day I am usually alone at home working on my paintings, although I doubt I would ever be good enough to get something in one of those fancy upscale galleries. Okay, so I've never tried but still... I was happy with my life and never missed any of those things most people had. I did not want to get married and have kids. I did not want the house on an acre of land with a white picket fence and large maple tree out front. I just wanted to paint and live my life.

Being born and raised in the low income areas of Queens, NY, I know my place and I am happy with it. I've never been one of money so I have never been a target for crime. I always dressed appropriately in public so I was less of a target for sexual predators. You would be more apt to see me in paint covered sweat pants and a baggy tee shirt than skin-tight jeans and tank top. I was a good girl growing up and always stayed out of trouble. I knew how to go unnoticed and how to survive on these streets, or so I thought. All my life I have felt safe and secure within these neighborhoods... Until today...

Have you ever been hurt so bad by someone you wish you were dead?
Or perhaps your pain was so deep you wished they were dead?
I have known pain like this and I will do something about it.
Hurt no more, fear no more, cry no more.
Revenge is sweet and it is mine.
-back of a sketch in Aingeal's book

Chapter 1

The sun's rays beat upon my face coaxing me to consciousness. Slowly, I try to open my eyes and although the left one opens, the right one will not and I can feel the swelling preventing it. My hair is plastered around my face, neck, and shoulders and it feels crusty and cold on my skin. I try to call for help, but my jaw is either dislocated or broken and when I try to open it, pain shoots throughout my face and neck, radiating from my jaw. Shivering, goose bumps spread over my bare dew covered skin. Even with the sun beating upon me, the morning is chilly and the dampness brings on a deeper level of cold. Shivering only increases the burning sensation that seems to be covering every inch of my body. Slowly I reach up with my left hand to feel my throat and it takes all my effort because my muscles are extremely sore. As my arm moves into my blurred vision, I see the abrasions around my wrists and suddenly the memories come flooding back. They crash into me like a great wave of fear and I remember being bound by a coarse rope. Frantically my mind goes back in time to how it all began...
***

I was preparing for working the evening shift down at the bar as usual. Braiding my long red hair and then twisting it around my head like a crown, I finish it off by clipping it with a silver and blue gemstone dragonfly. I still had the figure of an eighteen year old, including the small breasts, which did not bode well for big tips, so I wore my extra padded bra to give me a couple more cup sizes. I covered it with a tight-fitting short sleeve black tee with the bar's logo on it and finished the outfit with a pair of tight-fitting acid washed jeans and my thigh-high black boots. The boots were my favorite part of the whole outfit, as they were leather and laced up the back. They took some work to get into but they looked great and accentuated my long legs. I took one more look in the full length mirror before throwing on my leather jacket, shoving my wallet into my back pocket, grabbing my keys, and heading out the door. I turned to lock all the locks on my door and then headed to the stairs at the end of the hall. Although I lived on the third floor I was terrified of the elevator ever since I was stuck in it for over an hour the previous year when the power went out, so now I take the stairs. At the bottom of the stairs I turned left and skipped through the foyer. There, I am greeted Betty who as always sat in an old rocking chair near the front door knitting.

Betty replied with her usual "Evening Ain-jail dear" in a thick Southern drawl without even looking up from her work.

As she sits there, the knitting needles clacked furiously against each other as her old wrinkled hands worked at their task. I often wondered how someone so elderly could still have such dexterity in her hands, and I stopped a moment to appreciate her work.

"Beautiful" I exclaimed and she gives me a big smile as I head toward the front doors.

Opening the door of the building, I was greeted by a gust of cool fall air. It was a clear night and I loved the crispness the air seemed to have this time of year. Happily, I hopped down the front steps and turned right when I reached the bottom, heading down the sidewalk. At the end of my building, there is an alley that heads back to the parking lot. Sitting in the alley was a dark figure. He was hunched down, huddled in an old tattered black blanket, holding his hand out for spare change. This was not a new site for me as there was usually at least one or two of them huddled in the dark alley in the evenings, begging for spare change. They used the alley for security and shelter, especially if it is windy out. As always, I offered the homeless person three dollars which was how much the corner deli asked for a sandwich, chip, and drink combo. When he accepted the money, I made the suggestion he gets the meal and he thanked me as they always do. I knew that there was a fifty-fifty chance he would use the money for a forty ounce beer instead of the food, but at least I tried. I headed down the block toward the intersection and heard the man start to follow, his shuffling feet obvious in the silence of the night. Smiling at the thought he was going for the food instead of the beer, since the liquor store is the opposite direction, I felt that tonight would be a good night. As I reached the intersection I turned left onto W 6th Street and as always, several of the lights were out down this block. I did not live in the best of neighborhoods, some would even say it was one of the worst, but I did not mind it. I no longer heard the man's footsteps and figured he turned into the deli, so I continued down the dark street, unaware I was still being followed. Midway through the darkest section, I neared the old Cadillac. I did not remember seeing this one here the day before and I wondered if a new pimp moved in to the neighborhood. With a sad sigh and a shake of my head, I cautiously approached it. Generally when a new Cadillac with heavily tinted windows showed up, that was why. And it was usually followed by numerous visits from the local NYPD. My friends always told me I should move away from this area, but I liked living within walking distance of my job; it made it cost efficient and with the extremely high prices of gas these days, that was important. Besides, riding the bus or train at this time of night was no safer really. As I reached the front bumper of the car, I suddenly felt a presence behind me, but before I could turn, a hand with a rag came around and covered my mouth. There was an odd smell for the briefest moment and then the world started to go black.

When I came to, I found myself in one of the old factories down by the bay. I could tell where I was by the sounds of seagulls and ships, and the smell of the ocean; salty and fishy. Looking around, I saw cracked and painted windows and there was graffiti on some of the walls. Old rotten crates mingled with newer crates, and garbage was littered all around me. Looking up, I saw my wrists bound together and looking down, my feet were also bound by a coarse, thick rope. I was suspended above the ground from a big hook at the end of a long chain, like the ones used to hang animal carcasses in meat factories. There was also some sort of coarse fabric in my mouth and tied tightly around my head, so that it dug into the sides of my mouth and cheeks, causing searing pain. I was shivering from the cold because whoever took me, removed my clothes. Frantically, I scanned the area for my clothing but when I was unable to find them, I began flailing back and forth the way one would on a swing, trying to build up momentum. I was hoping to slide off the end of the hook or at least cut through the ropes binding my wrists, but only accomplished digging the rough ropes into my wrist more causing even more pain. Soon after I gave up and settled down, a man walked in. Or at least I assumed it was a man by his build. He was large but not fat; it was more muscle and he was quite tall with a squared frame. He was dressed all in black, including butcher's gloves that reached his elbows. The only thing that was not black was the white doctor's mask over his lower face and butcher's apron. His head was covered by the hood of his hoodie, putting his upper face and eyes in shadows. He walked toward me slowly as if he were studying me, tilting his head slowly to the left and then to the right. There was an old doctor's case in his left hand, and his right hand clutched tightly and released slowly, over and over in anticipation as it hung down at his side. When he nearly reached me he set the case down on one of the intact crates a couple feet away from me and quickly closed the gap between us. He ran the fingertips of his right hand over my face, gently moving downward, carefully tracing the muscle of my neck. He caressed my shoulder and flowed down to the outside of my breast, to my side, ending on my hip. It was not necessarily sexual, almost as if he were checking for defects in a piece of furniture, but the way he peered into my eyes as he touched me, sent terror down to my very core. He slowly moved behind me, sliding his hand across my stomach and then running his hand around my waist and up my spine. He stopped at the back of my neck, sliding his fingers around it and gripping it lightly. Gently, he pulled my head back and I could feel his breath on my ear.

With a gravelly voice he whispered, "I am going to make you suffer slowly and then I will have my way with you until you wish for death, but do not worry; I will not take your life. I am not a murderer."

The way he said it, the emphasis on the last part of the sentence, it was as if he truly believed, as long as I stayed alive, he was not doing anything wrong. He then let out a horrible, dry laugh that sent a chill up my spine. I started flailing frantically hoping to escape him, and his grip on my neck loosened but I still felt his breath against my ear for a moment longer and then it was gone. He came back into my view and walked over to the case on the crate. Opening it, he pulled out a syringe and held it up for me to see. The tip of the needle is capped and there is a clear thick liquid in it.

"If you keep flailing like that, I will be forced to use this and it will paralyze you so you cannot move any more but you will still feel everything. Is that what you want?"

I stilled myself, knowing that if he used that on me, I would have no chance of escape. At least this way, I have a chance.

He reached back into the case and pulled out a small silver and black box with several knobs on it. There were wires attached to one side of it, bundled up, and little hooks on the ends of the wires. Panic struck and I was unable to help myself as I began flailing. He laughed that terrible laugh, setting the box down and picking up the syringe stalking toward me like a predatorily animal. He grabbed my side and held me steady as he jabbed the end of the needle into my skin. I felt growing warmth spreading out from where he pierced me, and within moments I could not move but I could still feel the sting of the injection point. Fear gripped me and I tried to squeeze my eyes closed but they would not cooperate. I watched as he walked back and set the needle down, picking up the strange box and returning to stand in front of me. As he stood there, he stared into my eyes and placed the box into the pocket on the front of the apron leaving both his hands free. He slowly untied the twist-tie binding the wires and then let the length drop while supporting the hooks in his fingers. With his left hand he held my right hip to steady me while he used his right hand to pierce the hook through the flesh just to the outside of my left breast. He gave my hip a slight caress before switching hands and doing the same thing on my right. After both hooks were in place, he caressed both my hips, sliding his hands up and down them before turning me slightly from side to side to examine his work. Tears streamed down my face and a small trickle of blood did the same from each puncture point. I was lucky the barbs had been filed down on the hooks though, or there would have been more damage. He then took a small step back and reached into his pocket for the box. Holding it in his left hand he used his right to flick a switch on the top and then turn one of the knobs as a small electrical current started to stream out of the hooks and into my sides. I tried to scream or move, but no sound came out and my body was still but for the slight shaking the electric was causing it to do, and my eyes threatened to roll back into my head. I was helpless and he made my breathing come in ragged gasps with the fluctuation of the current as he turned a second knob up and down. My body reacted to the electricity in ways which would bring me nightmares if I survived. When he was satisfied with the results he unclipped the wires from the hooks and caressed my breasts, enjoying the reaction he brought forth. With a satisfied sound he turned away and went back to the bag. He pulled several more items of torture out of it and laid them carefully on the crate, showing me each one before placing it down. The next item he chose to use on me looked like a piercing gun and when he pulled out a packet of hoop earrings and placed them in the pocket of his apron, open side up, it confirmed my fears. With the gun in hand, he walked around me and ran his free hand from my shoulder to my buttock, cupping it and giving a little squeeze. His hand then moved back up and I felt him pull out the skin on my back, just below the shoulder blade on the left side and then there was a sharp pain and a loud click noise before the feeling of the hoop being fed through my raw flesh into the newly-made hole. He continued the process putting three more rings in a line down to just above my butt cheek, and then he repeated the pattern down the other side. After he placed the last ring he went back to the case and pulled out two coils of metal wire and slowly walked back behind me, unrolling the wire as he went. I felt him lacing the wire through the hoops, a slight tugging as he pulled the wire through them. He started at the bottom right and ended at the top left. There was a soft click sound and then I felt the tug of him clipping the wire to the hook still in my side. He then laced the second wire the same way through the rest of the rings. The ends of the wires hung down, tickling the backs of my knees. He walked back over to the crate and picked up the little electrical box and returned, facing me this time.

"I want to watch your reaction to this… oh wait you can't react" he said, and then laughed that evil laugh as he attached the clamps on the box to the ends of the wires, letting them brush against my hips.

I could feel the electricity move across my hips, up through the hoops, and into the hooks at the top. The voltage was low enough not to burn my skin, but it felt like fire at each of the points where metal pierced my flesh. Tears streaked my face yet again, and my body twitched with the electrical charge slithering up the wires. He laughed as he slowly turned the little knob on the box up and down, the twitching becoming more violent as he went up, then easing as he lowered the voltage. He moved closer and slid his hand between my thighs, and I could see the mask on his face as he formed a smile beneath it. Tears were running down my cheeks and finally a soft whimper escaped my lips. He turned off the power and unhooked the box from the wires, shaking his head.

"It appears the drugs are wearing off, oh that is not good" he snarled as he went back to the case, extracting another syringe.

"Your body is enjoying it but your mind is fighting and we cannot allow you to hurt yourself."

Again he lets out that horrendous laugh as he returned to me. He went behind me and suddenly, I felt the jab of the needle in my neck and then watched him walk back to the bag. He must have tired of electricity, because the next thing he pulled out was an Exacto knife and a squirt bottle filled with some translucent yellow liquid. He walked back to me, bottle in his left hand, open blade in his right.

"It is amazing how much pain you can cause with the smallest cuts and a little citric acid" he said almost jovially.

He then proceeded to make several tiny flattened U shaped cuts down my ribs from the bottom of my breast to my belly button and then squirted the liquid down them. With the smell of lemon juice strong in the air, I wanted to scream but no sound came out. I wanted to flail and fight, but the injection had travelled through my system quite quickly, so all I could do was hang there and suffer in silence. He looked at my face as tears filled my eyes. He was pleased with the results thus far and started working down the other side making small cuts every couple inches and then spraying them with the lemon juice. When he started across my collar bone, I passed out. I was awakened to the force of cold water against my face; he was hosing me off with what looked like a fire hose to remove all the juice and blood that had crusted onto my skin. The pain was overwhelming as he sprayed me all over with the high powered water. With an angry grunt, he shut off the water off and used what looked like a car sponge and soap to scrub my body, careful not to rip out any of the souvenirs he left in me. I had a moment to notice the crate and all the tools were gone when he took the hose to me again. When all evidence was removed from my skin, he hosed down the entire area around me. The smell of bleach was heavy in the air and my skin burned even where he had not cut into it. He turned the hose off again and wound it up as he went out the door.

When he returned he growled "Your passing out has cut my fun short, you little bitch" and then he punched me across the face causing a surge of pain, and my jaw almost immediately started to swell.

I whimpered, the gag still in place, trying to beg for mercy but he hit me again, causing me to black out once more.
***

Now I am lying on the still damp ground beneath the area I so recently was hanging and prayed to be saved. I reach up again to touch my face and do not recognize what I feel. He had hit me pretty hard both times and who knew how many more after I was out. My face was severely swollen from the impact, but at least he had removed the gag and ropes that bound me. My neck and throat are extremely sore, although I do not remember him choking me. Who knows what he could have done to me while I was passed out, though. That thought panicked me more than anything, as I remembered his threat. What *had* he done to me while I was out? I felt down my body and every place I touched seared in pain, but as I felt between my legs, I realized he had not had opportunity to rape me. Perhaps the idea of doing it when I could not respond did not turn him on enough to complete his plan. Either way, I was happy to know that at least my virtue was intact, even if the rest of my body was battered and bruised.

Suddenly, I begin to smell smoke as the direction of the wind changes and blows a puff of it through one of the broken windows. With my one good eye, I try to look around for where it was coming from and notice there is a large fire outside. This means that help would be on the way, and I strain to listen for sirens. As I lay there, questions spin through my head. How long I had been out? Had he started the fire? Why? Is he still here somewhere? Then I heard them, the sirens off in the distance. Help io on the way; I am saved! Suddenly, panic grips me again, how will they know I am inside? I begin to struggle, forcing myself to roll over. I need to get closer to the door, closer to the outside where the firemen will be putting out the fire. With all my will, I am forced to drag myself, pulling my already cut up body, scraping along the rough cement floor as my legs do not seem to want to work. Tears streaming down my face as a hoarse cry finally escape my lips.

I hear a man's voice call, "There's someone inside!"

I hear the door being broken down and my last vision is of the fireman rushing in to save me. He is a bright blur of motion through the tears, and I see the look on the young man's face as he reaches down toward my broken and battered body. That look, the sadness will forever haunt my dreams, as my eyes roll back and darkness comes once again.

Chapter 2

Nightmares haunt my dreams. Darkness, filled with the look of pity and despair I saw on the face of the man that saved me just before the world went black, swirling images combine with the evil laugh of the evil man. While I drift in a medically-induced coma, my thoughts refuse to allow me the rest I need. Over and over, I relive the torture and the rescue, unable to escape it. Each time a nurse checks my IV or takes a blood sample, I feel the needles used by my tormenter, slipping into my skin as I lay there helpless. Each time they shine the light into my eyes, I see the morning sun shining through the windows. When they lift my body to change the sheets, I see my savior's face, lifting me from the rubble. Physically, I've suffered horrible trauma and my face required cosmetic and medical surgery to repair the broken bones in my cheek and jaw and hide the scars. The doctors worked diligently to repair as much of the damage as they could, rubbing salves into the abrasions and small cuts to minimize scarring. As my body lays there bruised and battered and healing slowly, I can sense someone sitting beside me like a lone guard. Even among the coming and going of all the other bodies, I can feel him. In my dreams, I can hear him off in the distance whispering my name but I think it is just more torture and dismiss it.

When they finally bring me out of the coma, I am blinded by the brightness in the room. Six weeks have passed while I healed in this hospital bed. The first person I see is my doctor, and the white mask over his face brings on a sudden and fierce panic attack. He is looking down at me and although my logic tells me I am safe, I am still on the verge of screaming in terror. My eyes go huge and my heart rate skyrockets, as I suddenly cannot breathe. I scramble up the bed trying to get away from him and the female nurse that was standing beside him rushes to my side. She carefully grabs me, settling me down. Realizing something is wrong, the doctor steps back and lowers the mask from his face briefly identifying himself as my doctor, and telling me I am safe now before returning the mask over his nose and mouth.

As he is doing this, the nurse gently caresses my shoulder and arm, telling me to take it easy and that everything is okay. She is using a soothing voice and making comforting sounds as the doctor apologizes yet again and keeps a reasonable distance while waiting for it to register.

I take a long blink and deep breath, slowly letting it back out. I look at the nurse, careful to avoid looking at the doctor and ask if the doctor could leave his mask off or even better just leave the room.

Unfortunately, for medical reasons, he could do neither as he is required to asses my vitals and inform me of the procedures I went through while under his care. He offers to stand outside of my view while he speaks with me and the nurse continues to sooth me by rubbing my arm gently and making soft pleasant noises.

I am unsure if it will even work, but when he moves to the doorway far from the bed, I feel slightly relieved. I turn away from him, allowing the nurse to somewhat cradle me, and I am able to get my heart rate back down to normal.

The doctor takes the opportunity to tell me about the surgery to my jaw and the cosmetic surgery to my face, as well as all the minor work that needed to be done.

He explains why they opted to put me in a medical coma for the past six weeks and tells me I am lucky they were able to repair everything "nearly good as new."

He then tells me he will return a little later when I am up to it and then I hear the door to my room open and close. The nurse nods when I look to her for assurance and then I look around the hospital room, searching for who might have been my constant companion but there is nobody else there, just me and my nurse.

Saddened, I lay back and looking to my left, I see some flowers on a table. I start to reach for the card, when there is a knock at the door. My hand hesitates, and as it opens without waiting for my response, I let it drop. I look at the officer in the doorway and he takes it as his cue, walking to the foot of the bed. His uniform is all wrinkled like he slept in it and there are dark circles around his eyes from lack of sleep.

"I am officer Pacitti, I have been assigned to your case" he states, looking down at me as one would an injured animal.

My first attempt to speak to him is hoarse and my throat burns with the effort. I could not understand why earlier I was able to speak just fine but now it was painful. Shaking my head I bring my hand to my throat and attempt to clear it. The nurse offers me a white Styrofoam cup with a bendy straw sticking out of the white plastic lid on it. I peek under the lid seeing it is filled with ice water and then sip slowly from the straw.

After a few small sips, I clear my throat again and then softly ask "Did you find him?"

His face saddens even more, making the lines around his eyes and mouth more pronounced, and he tells me they could not find anything on the scene to help with the search. He had destroyed any evidence and with the only witness in a coma, there has been no luck. He proceeds to ask me questions and is disappointed when I cannot describe the assailant with more than his physical build and voice, as well as what he was wearing. He tells me that they had nothing to go on and so they have been waiting for me to wake up so they could hopefully get some leads. He explains that the assailant had burned everything he used on the scene, destroying any evidence they may have been able to use.

I suddenly realize the man is still out there, possibly searching for his next victim or perhaps even waiting for me so that he can finish off what he started. There is nothing the police can do to stop him, because they have nothing to use to find him and my heart rate spikes again.

I yell "NO that can't be possible!" and the nurse rushes to my side and tries to calm me, but I shove her hands away and plead with the officer to tell me he was joking.

Saddened, he comes around the bed and takes my other hand in one of his, caressing it with the other. This calms me slightly, so he tells me that he has been working day and night, but has not had any luck and then he apologizes, backing up slowly as my hand slides from his. The officer thanks me and wishes me good luck, leaving his card on the table in case I remember anything, before he heads out the door. When he reaches the door he turns to me and seeing me lying on the bed, silent tears streaming down my face, he offers me his friendship as well as his protection.

I nod to him in a silent thanks and he exits the room.

Nurses come and go at regular intervals for the rest of the day. Each one checks my mental and physical state, looking over my wounds and speaking in soft comforting tones. I can see the look in each of their faces, the 'oh that poor girl' expression. After two stressful incidents, they wanted to keep me as calm as possible, and instated a "no visitors" rule on me for a couple days until I am able to maintain a stable level of security. There were no more visits from the male doctor after the mere suggestion of him visiting raised my heart-rate. Instead I was reassigned a tall thin female doctor with cold grey eyes and shockingly white hair that did not match her youthful features. She keeps her hair pulled into a tight bun at the nape of her neck, giving her a slightly menacing look which is offset by the warm smile on her face.

She introduces herself as Doctor Randal and does a complete physical exam of me. She shines a light into my eyes, leaving spots in my vision for the rest of her visit. She puts light pressure on my jaw where it hinges and asks me to open and close my mouth slowly. The entire time she works, she is focused on her job but keeps that warm smile. When she is finished, she asks if I have any questions or need anything. When I tell her I am fine and thank her, she lets me know that the nurses are only a button push away and heads out the door.

The rest of the morning is nurses in and out. Eventually I tire of all the commotion and ask a small portly nurse named Jean if it is all really necessary.

Jean gives me a look that says "What do you think" as she explains how long I was out and that it is procedure to ensure there were no complications.

She reminds me of my reactions to both the doctor and the officers' visit and I sigh, succumbing to the tiresome visits.

Eventually, I am able to block them out as my mind turns to trying to remember something, anything that might help catch that evil man. I then remember the flowers and carefully reach for the card, trying not to pull on the tube still running to my arm. When I pull it off and get it into view, I see it is a generic flower shop card with some ribbon and balloon graphics adorning it.

In the center of the card in neatly handwritten cursive it reads "Aingeal, here is hoping for a fast recovery. ~D~" I wonder where it came from and a shiver of fear runs through me.

Of course, this also happens to be the one time I am not being harassed by one of the many nurses. I consider using the little button they explained was for emergencies but decided it was not worth getting into trouble for on my first day. Well not really my first day because I've been here forever but... Almost on cue the door opens and a nurse enters with a tray in her hands.

"I've brought you dinner. Fair warning, it's pretty bland and mushy but they want to be careful since you've not had solid food in weeks."

The nurse then pulls an adjustable table over and moves it in place in front of me, where she uncovers the tray and sets the cover beside it. I take one look at the unappetizing and unrecognizable mush in the bowl and cover it back up. With a laugh the nurse uncovers the tray again and reminds me that I need to eat.

I offer the nurse a deal, "If you can tell me where the flowers came from, I will eat this mush you gave me."

The nurse tells me they were delivered by the hospital florist and that she will ask and then points at the bowl. I sigh and then holding my breath, I take a spoonful of the goop. When it touches my tongue I gag, as the texture is a combination of sand and Fluff, that marshmallow gooey stuff you spread on a sandwich. It feels like I am eating pond scum and it tastes about the same. It takes me quite a while and several episodes of gagging to get the bowl down but then I am given a cup with some apple juice to wash the nastiness down. With a full belly, I am shocked to feel myself becoming increasingly drowsy. This is when the nurse explains that a coma is not the same as sleep and that I should try to rest. With that, I let my eyes drift closed and slowly the darkness of sleep envelops me.
***

The next two weeks healing in the hospital are about the same. Watching and waiting for another sign from this mysterious 'D'. Doctor Friedmann, my assigned psychiatrist, visits me daily since I was brought out of the coma, but I realized it has been three days since his last visit. As I am pondering his absence, he walks in as if on cue with a young man at his side. I immediately recognize the face; it is the fireman that found me in the building. I remember seeing it every night in my dreams, as he carries my off to safety.

The Doctor introduces him as Aidan Dooley or Dean as his friends call him.

As he stands in the doorway he is slightly leaning against the frame and smiling hopefully. I wonder why he is here but unable to drum up the courage to ask, so I just look at him and a thought springs to mind. What if he is the mysterious "D" from the flowers? Out of his uniform Dean is still well built, but then one would need to be in order to be a firefighter. He has shortly cropped auburn hair and green eyes with a hint of freckles on his cheeks, very Irish I think as I fight a smile, losing in the end. He is wearing well-fitting blue jeans and a forest green tee shirt that makes the color of his eyes more noticeable. In his right hand he has a small teddy bear holding a balloon that says "GET WELL" on it; in his left hand he carries a pot with a brightly colored metallic wrap around it tied with a red bow. In the pot are some burgundy Gerbera Daisies in full bloom. Looking from the pot, to Deans face to the Doctor,

I finally gets the nerve and ask "Why the visit?"

Doctor Friedmann proceeds to tell me that Dean spent a lot of time at my side since I was admitted two months earlier, keeping me company even though the doctors said it was not necessary. I wonder if he is who I sensed all this time and if that was why he invaded my dreams so often. I am confused by this, however, and ask why he bothered. Dean takes this as an invitation to move a little closer and he hands the gifts to me as he tells me why.

"When I found you there you were so broken, but I saw the fight in your eyes. There was a trail of blood several yards long from you to the door and I realized you must have dragged yourself. I was amazed by your willpower and had to get to know the person you are…"

He trails off because of the confused look on my face and the increase in the beeping of my heart monitor. He gently touches the tips of his fingers to my cheek and then moves his hand away.

As my heart rate slows back down he continues "…I sat there (nodding toward the chair) waiting for you to wake up, and after the first couple days, I started talking to you, hoping you would hear me. I read to you and told you about what was going on in the news. When the doctor told me I was your only visitor I was secretly relieved, hoping you were single…" and then he blushes.

I reach out and take his hand, then thank him. I knew that I would not have many visitors but it saddened me that not one of my friends could visit, but instead I was kept company by a complete stranger.

After a few moments of silence, Doctor Friedmann tells me that I am to be discharged today and Dean offers to take me home.

I accept his offer graciously; unsure why I am since I do not even know him, but since I have nobody else, I figure I might as well. I then realize I arrived at the hospital nude and wonder what I will be wearing to leave.

As if reading my mind Dean tells me that he got me some sweatpants, a sweatshirt, socks and panties. He had asked the head nurse in charge of me, Betty, about my size so he hopes they will fit.

I smile at him and thank him again for his kindness, although I am still wondering what he wants from me, distrust barbed deep in my soul after what I went through.

Just then Nurses Mary and Gene enter and tell the men it is time for them to give my some privacy while they do a final exam and help me dress to go. Dean smiles and gives me a cowboy salute, tipping his invisible hat. Doctor Friedmann tells me he will return when I am dressed to set up a schedule for the next few weeks and turns to leave.

As the men close the door behind them, I ask the nurses for a mirror. I have not been able to see myself since the ordeal and I want to see how bad it looks. Nurse Mary pulls a compact out of her pocket and hands it to me. I hold up the mirror and see that there are two thin pink scars on my face. One is along my left cheek bone and the other down the right side of my jaw. Gently, I trace each scar as silent tears slide down my face and then I remember the rest of the damage and frantically starts pulling the blankets and gown off. I look down and find faint crescent shaped pink lines down my front and after trying to twist to see my back, ask about rings that were forced into the skin.

Nurse Gene tells me that they removed the rings because of the tearing and the holes healed well only leaving tiny round scars at each of the sites.

Nurse Mary wraps me in a blanket, pulling me in for a hug and that is when I realize I have been crying.

Several hard sobs escape and then I close my eyes, take in a deep breath, and regain my composure.

Nurse Gene approaches with the royal blue sweats that Dean bought for me and begins to help me put them on. After I am dressed I look at my feet clad in hospital socks and Nurse Mary offers me slippers while she explains that Dean forgot to get me shoes.

I give a short laugh, thanking Mary and putting the footwear on as Nurse Gene goes to retrieve the men.

Dean walks in first, a smile spreading across his face as he sees me in the outfit he bought for me and blushing when he reaches my feet. "

Sorry about the shoes, but you look comfy," he says as he walks up and takes my hands.

I jump at his touch and then grip his hand when he tries to pull away. I explain that I must be jumpy still and he smiles and rubs his thumb across my knuckles soothingly.

Nurse Gene asks Dean to step aside so she can help me into the wheelchair. As she does this, Dean goes around the room with a box they gave him at the nurses' station and gathers up the assorted gifts he had dropped off over the past few weeks. When he is done, he gently sets them in my lap.

Doctor Friedmann sits down on the chair next to the bed and opens his appointment book on his lap and looks at me, "Time to set up our schedule for the next couple weeks, young lady" he says as he clicks his pen open. He gives me a stern look as he states "I don't want you going back to work for at least that long" and he goes on to explain why.

I nod and we proceed to set up my schedule, planning for one in-home visit alternating with one office visit every two days. Doctor Friedmann wants to be sure that I am coping at home, but he also wants to be sure that I am able to comfortably leave the home as well.

With that, I say goodbye to the doctor and my nurses, and then Dean takes up point behind me pushing me out the door.

While we are waiting in the elevator he must have realized he does not even know where to bring me and with a nervous laugh, asks where I lives.

I tell him my address and realize suddenly that I no longer have my keys and worry that my apartment might not be safe. Frantically, I ask if anyone found my keys and Dean tells me that Officer Pacitti mentioned something about them finding the remains of my purse and jacket in the rubble of the bonfire, including what was most likely my keys. At least I know that "he" does not have them, now I just have to hope the landlord or his son is around to let me in.

As we approach the desk, I realize that I am also missing my ID and medical cards but the nurse tells me that it is all taken care of and that they were able to get my information, so I am all set to leave.

Dean wheels me through the first set of doors and leaves me next to Joe at security, telling me he needs to run out and pull his car around. With a kiss on the top of my head, he is out the door before I have a chance to respond.

As I sit there patiently waiting while staring at the closed doors, Joe gives me a smile and starts making small talk.

I was never one for small talk, but right now I find it comforting as it takes my mind off the future. As Joe starts to talk about the scores for the latest sports game, I see a 1968 navy blue Chevy Impala SS pull up to the doors and my jaw drops. It is in perfect condition and the sunlight gleams off the hood as it comes to a stop. I figure he must have recently washed it, since it was perfectly spotless. Dean jumps out of the drivers' side and quickly comes in to wheel me out the electric doors.

I give Joe a quick goodbye as I exit the hospital and am wheeled up to the amazing car before me.

I ask him how he managed to be lucky enough to own that car and he tells me that it was his grandfather's, and proceed to tell me that he was raised by him after his parents were killed in an apartment fire. That is why he became a fireman, to save others the pain of losing a loved one.

I request a quick ride around the car so I can see the entire thing, and after the tour, he lifts me out of the chair with such ease I wonder just how much muscle was under that shirt. Feigning to slightly lose my balance, I place my hand on his chest and feel the muscles beneath his shirt. Gently setting me in the passenger seat with a big grin on his face, he closes the door and then he returns the chair.

As he opens the driver's door, he tells me "Let's get you home!"

Settling nicely into the driver's seat, he closes his door and starts her up. Pulling away from the curb, the engine purrs like a content kitten. I comment on how nice the engine sounds and Dean just grins. I can tell he is very proud of the car, and when I am feeling better I plan to check it out a little more closely. Closing my eyes, I lean back into the seat and try to relax, but I am so anxious about my return home that I just sit there with a tenseness I cannot shake.

Chapter 3

The rest of the trip is spent in silence, Dean is pretending to concentrate on the road and I am lost in my thoughts. It is not until we pull up to the front of my building I realize I forgot to tell him to go around back to the parking area.

I give him directions to go around the block to the driveway and pull into the big lot behind the row of buildings. There is a large lot tucked in the center of the block and as we reach the rows behind my building, I point to the section under the '3' sign and tell him to park in the spot marked 'E' since that is my personal spot. I do not own a car, so the spot is empty and he gives me a quick sideways glance before pulling in. He looks around somewhat concerned so I tell him that the parking area directly behind my building is well lit. I also point to the surveillance cameras covering the entire lot and tell him there is twenty four seven surveillance so it is the safest place for him to park such a nice car.

He thanks me for the thoughtfulness and then gets out first and runs around the car to get my door to help me out. I shoo away his hand and with a little struggle, I am finally able to exit the car on my own. He shakes his head at my stubbornness, but gives me the room I need to get out on my own. He closes my door and he offers to take my arm, but I shake my head no and start walking to the building.

As we approach the back door of my building, Tommy, the elderly security guy, opens it on cue. During the day it is his job to watch the monitors in the security room and normally he just buzzes people in the back door. Today however, he greets us at the door and asks if I am okay.

He offers his sympathy for what I had gone through and tells me the generic "If there is anything you need" speech followed by a quick gentle hug.

I smile and thank him and then I introduce him to Dean. Tommy gives a quick hello to Dean, eyeing him like an overprotective father.

He then tells me that Ronny, the super's son, had the locks changed on the apartment for me and he hands me a key ring with the new keys on it.

"Ronny was worried about your safety and paid for the new locks himself after his stingy father refused to change them" Tommy said proudly.

Tommy has worked with the building since his twenties and has known Ronnie since he was a newborn just coming home. He has given him much of the compassion and understanding that he has now, since his father was never around to do the job himself. Tommy always thought ahead, to the day when Ronny would eventually take over his father's job as super, and he wanted to be sure the boy would be kind and fair, unlike his father. I am glad of Tommy's influence and I will sleep better knowing that there are new locks on my door.

With keys in hand Dean starts leading me toward the elevator just down the hall and when I hesitate, he asks if everything is okay.

I explain my fear of elevators to him and with that he lifts me off my feet before I can even protest and whooshes me up the stairs toward the third floor. About halfway between the first two floors, I start yelling at Dean about how I am perfectly capable of walking and to put me down, but he just laughs and gets a tighter grip on me before continuing. When he reaches my floor, he heads through the fire door and stops. I give his shoulder a hard smack and when he still refuses to put me down, I point to the right. He heads down the hallway, stopping in front of the door with 3E in tarnished letters on it. Setting me down at the door, he takes a quick look around. When I give him an odd questioning look, he explains he was noting the exits and windows in case of an emergency, and I smile at his ever professional behavior and wonder if he is always like this, or if it is just because of his concern for me. I look down at the key-ring and there are four keys on it. I note there are two distinct pairs and I try the smaller key in the top lock first, and when it does not work, I try it in the other one and hear it clicking unlocked. I then use the larger key in the top lock; this one is the bar that goes across the door and the frame making it nearly impossible to kick the door open. You could try but the most you would do is bring the top of the door down on your head and the police on your heels. I stand there for several moments, looking at the door with my hand on the knob. I am not sure I am ready to go in, but then Dean reaches over and takes my other hand giving it a squeeze, and it gives me the courage to open the door.

As I open the door, I look down the hall that leads into my apartment. I look as the hall passes by my bathroom and kitchen leads into the living-room. There is a faint staleness to the air from it being closed up so long and make a mental note to open a few of the windows, as well as let out a sigh of relief knowing my apartment had not been opened in a while. I look in to my right at my bedroom and I am glad to see the door closed as well. It keeps it warmer in there in the winter and the fact it is still closed means it is unlikely anyone entered it while I was away, since I closed it when I left that night. As I walk into the apartment, I lead Dean in by the hand, more for comfort than guidance. My heart is racing now but the knot that had been in my chest the entire ride home is starting to ease. It fades away completely as I lock the two locks on the door as well as the chain at the top, giving me a sense of security. I check in my room briefly before leading him down to the living-room, checking the kitchen as we walk by it. I release his hand and motion him toward the couch and then I start to open the windows. As I lift the window open, I check the gates on the outside to ensure they are secure. Dean looks around, following me as I take stock of the apartment. I continue opening windows and checking gates as well as looking for anything that might be out of place.

When we reach my room I put my hand on his chest, stopping him from following me in. He nods and smiles in understanding, waiting in the doorway for me to finish. As he walks down the hall following behind me back to the living-room, he looks at the paintings I decorated the walls with. About halfway down he notices they all have my signature on them. When he reaches the living room he takes another look around and sees the wooden box tucked behind the couch. Walking up to it he smiles at the paint fingerprints and spatters on it.

"I didn't realize you paint" he calls to me.

I respond with something about stress relief and doing it only when I have the time.

Realizing I had not followed him, he wanders back down the hall to meet me. He finds me in the kitchen, cleaning out the refrigerator. I have the garbage can to the side of the open door and I am just throwing things into it. Looking at me, he wonders if I will be okay alone tonight. He takes a menu off the refrigerator for Peking Kitchen, a nearby Chinese restaurant that delivers to my area and smiles.

He sees that I have several things circled and after asking if I am hungry and getting a definitive "YES", decides to order something for us to eat.

When I give him a questioning look he tells me it is on him and that I can consider this their first date. He laughs to add a lighthearted note to it and then starts to dial the phone.

Well you owe me a movie, too" I tease as I throw away a plastic container with a mystery black goo in it that sloshes around like something out of a horror movie as it lands in the can.

With a laugh and a nod, he puts in the order, adding a couple items to the ones I circled. Once he hangs up, he comes over and starts looking at the magnets on the door of the refrigerator as I continue to clean out the inside of the fridge with 409 and a whole roll of paper towels. He makes some comments as I scrub at the fridge, trying to remove the stench. All my food had spoiled while I was in the hospital, leaving behind a putrid mess.

After I finish cleaning out the fridge to my satisfaction, I go over to the counter and after giving it a quick wipe-down, I start a pot of coffee. Good coffee was the one thing I missed the most, and I was going to drink a lot of it even without my favorite liquid creamer. Luckily, I keep a stash of the powdered stuff for just such an emergency. Once I am done setting up the coffee maker, clicking the little on button to green, I start cleaning off the rest of the counter with the 409. Laying out a kitchen towel, I wash a couple of mugs and set them on it to dry as well as a spoon. Normally I am not such a clean freak, but after over a month of the apartment being empty I feel I am justified in going a little overboard with my cleaning in here. I am about to justify myself to Dean, when I notice him wiping down the table for me. With a smile on my face, I go back to work.

As I am finishing up sweeping, there is a knock at the door that causes me to jump and smack my elbow into the wall.

After a quick look at my elbow, Dean offers to get the door, stating it is probably the food anyway.

I watch him leave the kitchen and soon hear low talking at my front door as the apartment is filled with the smell of Chinese food. I pull out the Ziplock bag of paper plates from the upper cabinet over the sink and set them on the table just as he walks in.

I excitedly exclaim "I sure hope they remembered to put in the chopsticks!" and Dean looks at me a little concerned.

He confesses that he does not know how to use chopsticks and I giggle before pulling out a fork and washing it off. As I do this, he starts pulling out the white cartons of food setting them on the table. I open each one, smelling the delicious aroma pouring out. After the hospital food, this looked like a feast. There is white rice to go with the sweet & sour chicken and the pepper steak with onions. He also got beef fried rice and wonton soup for the sides, and completed the meal with a couple egg rolls and fortune cookies. After unloading all the cartons, he dumps out the chopsticks, napkins and sauces from the bag.

We proceed to eat in silence with the occasional "Could you pass the" every now and then.

Once we are done with the meal, Dean tells me that I need food in the house because I cannot live off take out and leftovers and then offers to take me to the store.

I pour myself another mug of coffee and with a shrug say "Maybe after I finish my coffee.. and change… and maybe even get a shower."

I am not ready to go out yet but I do not want to tell him that, it would make me look weak and I do not want to look weak. I was weak once and that is how I got hurt, but not again. He smiles, showing he understands my hesitance and shoves a forkful of fried rice in his mouth.

When we have had our fill, Dean offers to clean up the table so I pull out some plastic containers and baggies for the leftovers.

We then walk into the living-room together. I have my coffee in one hand and his hand in the other and I feel content for the first time since I woke up. I just cannot understand this feeling of security I am feeling, but decide to worry about it later. Right now, I just want to enjoy it. He sits down on the couch pulling me down beside him and looks at the television.

Jokingly, he exclaims "You know we will have to go out if you want that movie!"

I attempt to glare at him as he grins back at me chasing the glare away. Finally I sigh "You're right, we need to go out and get some stuff."

Leaning back, coffee still in my hand, I close my eyes and take a deep breath letting it out slowly. Opening my eyes I take a gulp of my coffee, set it down on the forest green ceramic coaster and stand up.

"Give me a minute to get changed, I can always grab a shower when we get back" I announce as I head to my room, closing the door behind me.

Several minutes later I emerge and call to him "Let's go then" I say as I stand next to the front door.

I am resolved to get it over with quick and painless like removing a bandage that has been on too long. Unfortunately, bandage removal is never painless no matter how quickly you rip it off. Just as we are about to head out the door I realize the windows are all open. I ask Dean to help me close and lock them before we go. He heads back to the living-room while I start in my bedroom. He is coming out of the kitchen as I am getting there, so we walk out together.

Before heading down the hall I give the doorknob a jiggle and tug to be sure the locks were in place and gave him a "Don't you dare" when he attempted to carry me down the stairs.

The first place we hit is the Video-Rama just down the street to rent some movies for the night. Dean heads for the Action movies and I head for the New Releases and immediately grab the latest "Saw" movie. I was so looking forward to seeing it in the theater since it was being released in 3D, but that plan was bashed by my stay in the hospital.

When Dean questions my choice, I state that I have watched them all and nothing will stop me from seeing the last one.

In the back of my mind however a little voice whispers the first thoughts of revenge and ideas. I am thrown off by these thoughts, and immediately file them away. I will not let anything ruin this night. I then look at the movies he selected and pick on him about his obvious infatuation with a particularly large breasted actress.

After causing him to blush the entire walk from New Releases to Action, I pick out my second choice and we head to the register. Dean takes my selections and pays for the lot of them since we agreed this would be considered our first date. After getting the movies, we head to Dean's so he can pack an overnight bag. I had asked if he would be willing to stay at my place for a couple days until I was settled back in and he happily agreed, although his enthusiasm waivered slightly when I informed him he would be sleeping on the couch which brought a laugh from me.

When we walk into his apartment, I cannot help but laugh as it is very much the typical bachelor pad. Not a single item that would give it the "woman's touch" could be found at first glance. I walk into the cramped but not too cluttered living room and as I attempt to sit on the couch, I notice a magazine poking up from between the far cushion and arm. As I lean over and to reach for it, Dean leaps from the bedroom door and yanks it out quickly, hiding it behind his back. I burst into laughter when I realize what sort of magazine it is. Face red, he rushes into the other room that I assume is the bedroom.

Sitting on the couch, I can see nearly the entire apartment and start to take a better look at everything. There is a full living-room which includes his home gym; filled with weights and other small equipment. Dean had separated it off slightly with a folding wall which was only partially folded back. Behind the couch are the bedroom and the kitchen. I decide to get up and take a peek into his kitchen since he's in the bedroom.

I am curious to see if the fridge is filled with beer like they are in the movies. Dean is the first guy I've really dated, since I was always so busy with work and painting, so I had no idea what to expect. I was somewhat surprised by cleanliness of the kitchen. Even the sink is empty and there is only a bowl, spoon and glass set to dry on a dish towel. I am impressed. Turning, I look back over at his gym area and decide to go play with the equipment while I wait. As I pass the fridge, I take a quick peek and am slightly disappointed by the lack of beer. With a little giggle, I head to the bench and sit down on it, my back to the outside wall facing the weights. Leaning forward, I attempt to pick up a weight but I am barely able to lift it.

I let out an expletive or two under my breath and then try again just as Dean emerges from the bedroom wondering why I am swearing.

Walking up behind me he places his hand on my shoulder and says "The doctor told you that you would be weak after being inactive for so long, and 50 pounds one handed is tough even for me sometimes."

I know the last was only said to make me feel better since he was able to lift and carry me earlier as if I weighed no more than a pillow.

He moves around the bench, leaning down to pick up a smaller weight and hands it to me and says "Try this one."

I take the weight and it is much better. He then demonstrates how to do a proper curl and leaves me to it while he goes back into the bedroom. I continue to do curls, alternating between arms until he returns. I ask if it would be okay for me to borrow the smaller weights for a bit and he nods and proceeds to grab a couple more small weights and this odd giant elastic rubber band looking thing that he informs me is for exercising with. He sets everything into a gym bag and brings it over to place it with his overnight bag.

He then turns and looks at me for a moment before deciding to invite me to his gym. He explains that he can get a free trial guest pass for me so that I can try it out and see if I like it. I look at him sideways and then agree; figuring I could use a little more muscle and the extra time with him might be nice.

With that, we head out the door and back down to the car and drive to the nearby grocery store. As we walk in the door, I explain that I have a system and I lay it out to Dean as I grab my cart. We then wind our way through the dry goods first, and then produce, meats, dairy and finishing with frozen foods. While in the dairy department I make sure to get a large bottle of the chocolate mint creamer and I also pick up some of the Columbian blend coffee since it is stronger and more likely to help me stave off sleep.

Dean had picked up a hand basket on the way in and was throwing little things like microwave popcorn, chips and other snacks into it.

I had to comment about how he stayed so fit while managing to eat like that. He laughs and tells me about his regular workout routine which gets him a wide mouthed "WOW".

I knew that he worked out from our earlier conversation but from what he just told me it was on the verge of obsession. Although it was no wonder he is so well built, if I lifted weights and ran the tread as much as he does, I would be too. Part of me hoped he would settle down a little on the working out now that we are together but part of me did not, because then he can keep me on track with my own routine. And then I realize I just considered us a couple for the second time today. How is it possible since I just met him? Even though I woke up alone in the hospital, he had been with me for quite a while when I was under and his presence must have made a really good impression on me. As we wait in line, I thumb through a couple of magazines while Dean looks over the candy selection as an artist would his brushes, finally deciding on a Snickers bar.

He offers me one as well, but I point to the 3 Musketeers instead.

He places both chocolate bars and the magazine I showed the most attention to in his basket and we checked out.

Dean offers to load the groceries into his trunk for me, as he can see I am quickly losing energy. Surprisingly I let him, and then we head back to my apartment.

Dean carries me up the stairs, this time without any complaints, and then unloads the groceries. I work on putting everything away with his help before we start working on preparing dinner. We agreed on a citrus chicken with steamed vegetables and rice, so I get to work making the glaze for the chicken while he cleans and prepares the vegetables. After the short time standing at the stove, I pull out the handy microwave steamer bags and sit down at the table. I take over working on the veggies, asking him to work on the chicken for me. After trimming the chicken, he places it in the pot with the cooled glaze, swishing the pieces around to get them well coated and then pours it all into the glass baking pan I left on the counter for it.

He places the pan and set it in the oven and then I tell him where to get the pot for the rice. Normally, I would have prepared the entire meal myself but I had overdone it and I was feeling the consequences. Once everything is cooking, we then sit and share random facts about each other as we wait for dinner to be ready.

After everything is done, we agree to take our food in and eat on the couch so we can start the movie marathon and I can be a little more comfortable. Dean puts in the action flick that I picked first since he did not think he would be able to eat while watching the "Saw" movie and it is only polite to play one of my choices first. We sit and eat our meal and then I cuddle into Dean since I am sore and tired and his warmth is comforting.

Before putting in the second movie, Dean makes some popcorn with the reasoning of "You can't watch a movie without popcorn" even though we were both still stuffed from dinner.

He returns from the kitchen with the microwave bag of popcorn and his water in one hand and a bottle of Pepsi in the other for me. We proceed to watch all three movies, although Dean falls asleep half way through "Saw", which may be why he chose to watch that one last. When "Saw" ends, I carefully lift Dean's legs onto the couch and cover him with a blanket.

Quietly, I go to my room, stopping briefly to check the locks on the front door. As I walk into my bedroom, I lightly close the door and begin to undress. At first I avoid the full length mirror on my closet door, but then I decide I need to face my demons so I walk up to it and take a good look at the scars on my body. The cuts on my ribs were nearly invisible as I run my fingers over them, and the piercing marks resemble pock marks. It is the scars from the ropes that are still visible, especially around my wrists where they are still a dark pink and smooth. Throwing on my robe, I quietly go into the bathroom to brush my teeth, wash my face, and brush my hair. When I am done, I plug in the nightlight I keep under the sink and shut all the lights off in the apartment before going back to my bedroom. I take off my robe throwing it over the back of the chair I keep next to my dresser and head over to my bed, where I sit and look at my scars one last time. With a heavy sigh, I crawl under the covers to go to sleep. Unfortunately sleep is not my friend and I am haunted by vague nightmares of the evil man. I see him standing in front of me, laughing that horrible laugh, looking into my eyes like he is trying to see into my very soul. Several times I wake, covered in sweat and stifling a scream.

Chapter 4

The next morning, I am startled awake by a knock on my bedroom door.

Groggily, I ask Dean what he wants as I reach for my robe. I hope I did not come off as too angry but I am not a morning person to begin with and the lack of proper sleep, combined with residual images from the nightmares has made me extremely cranky.

Hesitantly, he apologizes for waking me and then tells me that Officer Pacitti is at the front door and wants to speak with me.

I quickly jump out of bed, all traces of lack of sleep and those horrible dreams wiped away. I pull my robe closed and tie the belt tightly around it. I run to the front door, hoping he has a lead and is looking for assistance. As I rush past Dean, I ask him to throw on a pot of coffee and meet the officer at the open front door.

After locking the door back up, I invite him in and escort him to the living-room.

He shakes my hand at the door and then follows me down the hall. Once we reach the living room, he waits for me to sit. I choose the big comfy chair right next to the end of the couch where officer Pacitti is standing. He looks back down the hall, glances around the room and then sits down.

Dean soon returns from the kitchen and sits on the opposite end of the couch, leaving the manly one cushion space between them. Dean tells us the coffee is brewing and will be ready soon, then looks at me and asks if I mind if he stays.

I tell him I do not mind and then look at Pacitti. The look on his face makes my heart sink.

He can see the hope on my face disintegrate and drawing in a deep breath, he starts by telling me that the case has gone cold. With no evidence and no leads, they have nothing to go on and that is why he is here. He is hoping that coming home may have reminded me of something, anything that might help with the investigation. Perhaps I saw something unusual on my walk that night before I was accosted or remember a strange face as we drove down my street.

I tell him about the car, describing it in detail because I remembered checking it out as I walked by since I am a fan of fancy older cars and was also intrigued with the fact the owner had not tricked it out except for the heavily tinted windows. In this neighborhood, cars usually go through a total overhaul leaving them looking more like Frankenstein monsters than antique beauties. I also tell him about the homeless person and explain I never actually saw the face of the man but described where he was, how he was sitting and anything else I could remember from that night.

After we talk a little more, the officer thanks me for my time and promises to get back to me if he finds anything new, as well as check in on me from time to time.

With that, we stand and I escort him to the door seeing him out. As he moves outside the door, I ask if he wants me to go down and show him the spot, but he tells me it is unnecessary as he passed by it on his way in. Waving goodbye as he walks down the hall, I close the door, locking all the locks with a heavy sigh. Turning, I lean my back against the door and let out a longer sigh, followed by a brief sob of regret. Closing my eyes, I take several deep breaths and gather myself together. Suddenly I smell fresh brewed coffee and opening my eyes, I see Dean standing in front of me with a mug in his hands.

"I thought you might need this", he states offering it to me.

I force a smile and take a sip of the coffee, followed by another longer one and realized he was right; the coffee is making me feel better. I carefully push away from the door with my butt and head toward the kitchen, coffee in hand. The coffee is good but I need something more substantial in my stomach to calm the butterflies threatening to burst out of it.

Opening the fridge, I pull out the package of bagels and hold them up to Dean, who shakes his head no and I reply with a "Your loss."

I turn while ripping a bagel in half and put it in the toaster and then put the package away. When the bagel pops up,

I place it on my plate, grabbing the cream cheese I look at him and ask "How can you possibly not want a bagel?"

He laughs and says something about the cream cheese being fattening and I shake my head as I slather on the cream cheese with a "Yummmmm."

Dean laughs again and pulls out a box of generic wheat cereal and the quart of skim milk he bought to keep here. When I look at the milk with a screwed up face, Dean laughs again.

In the store yesterday we discussed my aversion to milk with a bluish tint to it "It just looks wrong!" I exclaimed as he put it in the cart.

I give Dean's milk one last look of disgust and then put the container of cream cheese back in the fridge. Walking to the counter, I lick the butter knife and set it in the dishwasher and then sit down to eat. Dean sits across from me with his bland bowl of cereal and we eat in silence until he finally comments on the deep furrow in my forehead. I tell him that I am worried about what that man might do and who he will hurt next.

Dean questions why I think he will hurt someone else, and I tell him about how much the man enjoyed it and that if someone enjoys something that much, they will do it again. Besides, I continue, he has gotten away with it. The police can't find anything to help catch him, so he is free and clear so what is to stop him from doing again.

Just as I throw my hands up in frustration, Dean's phone rings. It is the captain and Dean tells me he needs to go in to work for a while for an emergency meeting but that he will only be gone until three at the most.

I remind him Doctor Friedmann is coming at ten, so it should be okay. He kisses me on the forehead and gets his shoes and jacket on, heading out the door. I lock all the locks behind him. My hands rest on the big bar that runs across the door wondering how secure it truly is, and suddenly, tightness pulls in my chest and I shiver. I have to sit on the floor to keep from falling. Leaning back against the door, I cradle my legs against my body. I sit like this for a few minutes before I can get up and shake off the fear.

I can do this! I tell myself out loud, I will NOT be afraid! Banging my fist against the floor, I stand and go for more coffee.

Heading into the living-room, I pull my full-size easel from the closet and a fresh canvas. I also grab my large tackle-box of paints from behind the couch. Going into the kitchen, I retrieve my palette and brushes from their tray under the sink where I dry and store them. As I reach into my case, I start to automatically go for the blues and greens but then change my mind. I am not in the mood for bright and lively colors; I want darker, sadder tones today so I reach for the red, black, burnt umber and other deeper colors. I start with my wide brush and cover the canvas in a fury of black and burnt umber with flecks of red and then I take a smaller brush and create a flame-like effect around the sides and bottom, flicking the brush toward the center of the canvas. Suddenly, I stop and stare at the canvas and inspiration strikes. I grab the blow dryer and quickly dry the paint on the canvas and then reach into the box. Pulling out the white paint, I create a dove in the center of the canvas with a broken wing, drying the white and adding the details with each new layer. The entire painting only takes me a little over an hour to do and it is complete with my signature. Looking at the clock, I see I still have an hour before the doctor arrives so I take my brushes and palette into the kitchen and clean them off, placing them in their home beneath the sink. I then go in and put all my paints away, carefully cleaning any residue from my fingers off the tubes and tucking the box back behind the couch. I smile; painting always helps me feel better. The only thing left now was the easel with the painting, which I carefully move into my bedroom where it can finish drying before I tuck it away. I look down at my pants and notice I have paint all over them, so I quickly changes into another pair of jeans and drop the painted ones in the hamper. The clean jeans also have paint on them but it is faded so the doctor will hopefully think nothing of it. I check myself in the mirror for any traces of paint I may have left on my face, cleaning off a light smudge on my cheek and another off the tip of my nose. I would rather not have to explain where the inspiration for the painting comes from since, like all my work, it comes from places deep inside me.

Returning to the living-room, I do a final check and then I sit on the couch. Looking at the television I wonder if I should turn it on and then I see the toppled pile of mail. I decide to go through that instead. I throw the huge pile into the middle of the living-room floor and sit down next to it, Indian style. I start by sorting it into piles: bills, catalogs, magazines, junk and stuff from friends. The last pile only contained a couple items. After creating the smaller piles, I go in and grab the recycle bin, placing the largest pile, full of catalogs, into it. I grab the cutlass shaped letter opener from my desk and sitting back on the floor start working on the bills. I open the envelope, straighten out the bill, place it in front of me and then throw the envelope in the recycling. After doing this with the entire pile I go through and check each of the bills organizing them by both sender and date. I look at the amounts due and it appears someone was paying my bills while I was in the hospital. There are no PAST DUE notices but several "paid" statements in the pile. I am unsure who to thank and make a note to ask the doctor, as well as Dean, if they know who it might have been. I set aside the most recent bills; place the receipts in a pile to my left for filing and the rest to my right, creating a shred pile. Now I start on the junk mail pile, opening each envelope up and setting anything with my name or address on it in the shred pile throwing the rest of the filler and envelopes in the recycling bin in front of me. Once done with the bulk of the mess, all which is left is a tiny pile of cards and letters most likely from my friends. I grumble at the fact that they could not bother to visit me in the hospital but felt it necessary to send me something to save face. I take this pile and placed it back on the table with a little more force than I planned. I return the bin to the kitchen and set the receipts in my filing cabinet in a file for this year. I grab the bills and head to my desk where I keep my checkbook. Sitting down, I write checks to cover my latest payments and looks at the final balance in my checking account. When I am done, I realize I will need to go back to work, or at least find another source of income in the meantime because even with the couple thousand in my savings, it was not going to last long. I was definitely not ready to return to work though, so perhaps I can find another way to get some income until I am. Perhaps unemployment or some other state funded aid is available. I make another note for my appointment with doctor Friedmann and then set the stamped payment envelopes on the little table by the front door right next to the large clamshell holding my keys.

Just as I set them down, there is a knock at the door and I jump, letting out a surprised screech.

Doctor Friedmann immediately calls from the other side of the door, apologizing for startling me.

Letting out a short laugh and blushing because he heard me, I peek through the peephole to ensure it truly is the doctor, and let him in. I explain why I was startled and he tells me it is a normal reaction and not to worry. After shaking hands, I invite Doctor Friedmann into the apartment, locking the door behind him, and show him to the living-room. He sits down in the chair and glances around the room.

Always the gracious hostess, I offer him something to drink and he accepts a cup of coffee with two sugars and no cream. I excuse myself and leave the doctor to get us both some coffee, giving myself some time to gather my wits after that little jolt.

When I return, he comments on the sticky notes on the wall behind the couch.

I tell him I have always used that method to remember important tasks and he is impressed and told me such.

He continues to explain that it is not often he finds someone so organized. People who are well organized generally recover quicker because of their need to keep things in a neat and orderly manner.

I thank him for the compliment and support and ask if he might know who paid my bills while I was in the hospital. As I am asking, I take that note down, balling it up and tossing it in the small round wastebasket beside the couch.

He tells me he is unsure of the answer but that he would ask at the hospital when he returns, and he makes a note in his little book. I then grab the second note, holding it in my hand while I ask how I could possibly receive an income while on a mental health break.

Doctor Friedmann explains my options and tells me that he will have his office mail me the necessary paperwork, jotting that in his book as well.

Relieved, I thank him and explain my financial situation and I mention that I will not even have money for food if I do not get an income as soon as possible.

He tells me he understands completely and that he was surprised the hospital did not send any paperwork home with me or at least inform me of my options. The doctor then moves to questions about Dean using my financial situation as a good Segway. He asks how I feel about him. How much time have I spent with him since getting home? Does he make me feel safe? Do I intend to continue seeing him? Would I would be willing to accept help from him until I am able to attain assistance from the government?

Unsure I would be able to accept charity from anyone, I have a hard time answering the last question right away. After a pause, I realize that if it came down to asking for help or starving, that I would accept the help.

The doctor smiles and comments on my strong personality and then he tells me it is good I found someone I can trust, especially after all I went through and that I will have no issues learning to be self-sufficient again. As my first step, he advises me to go down to get my mail on my own today and when I appear visibly shaken by the thought, he offers to write a prescription for something to help with my nerves.

I panic and shake my head violently as I decline the offer of drugs. The doctor immediately realizes what has happened and attempts to repair it.

He explains that the medication just calms emotions and is not a physical relaxant but it does not change my mind; I was not going to take any drugs for any reason. This adamant refusal leads to a talk about the fears I might be feeling right now and what I am to expect over the next few days. He tells me it is acceptable to be afraid but that I cannot let that fear rule my life.

Doctor Friedmann's little buzzer suddenly goes off and he tells me that means our time for the day is up. He asks if there is anything else that I need to discuss today and when I tell him that I cannot think of anything, he stands to leave. I escort him to the door, unlocking each of the locks from top down and open the door for him.

He comments on the number of locks and I explain that I did not add any new ones; I just use all the ones that were there now.

He nods and comments on how it does not say much about the neighborhood if it requires that much security and then bids me a good afternoon before leaving.

As he takes a step he turns to me and says "Think about what I said and feel free to contact me at any time if you need to talk."

With that, he turns and walks down the hall.

Closing and locking the door behind him, I look down at the mail to go out and am reminded of my task to go down to the mail boxes in the lobby. I continue to look at the mail and then up at the door and then back down at the mail. The indecision I am feeling is slowly eating away at me and a headache starts to form at the base of my skull. Slowly a ribbon of fear starts to wind its way around me, gripping my throat and choking off my ability to breathe. As the panic attack builds, I slam my fists into the wall and the pain clears my thoughts. With a second slamming of my fists comes the anger. I am not going to be helpless! Anger is so much better than fear; anger will keep me focused. Holding onto that anger, I snatch the mail off the table, as well as my keys and stomp out of the apartment. Furiously, I lock the door behind me and head down the hall. How dare he leave me feeling like this! I am stronger than that. I start walking past the elevator as usual but then I stop. I slam my palm against the down button and then step back watching the lights change over the doors. Standing there with a scowl on my face, I am determined to beat all my fears before they beat me starting right here and right now.

When the doors open, I am greeted by Chuck from 4E. He notices the expression on my face and backs into the far right corner away from the buttons, giving me plenty of room in the elevator. I board the elevator and press the button to close the doors after seeing the first floor button is already lit.

Chuck quickly expresses his condolences for what happened to me and goes on to say that he is glad to see me out and about again.

The entire time, he is avoiding eye contact and fidgeting his feet. It was obvious something was bothering me and he was trying to avoid turning my anger on him, but he is one of those people that cannot stand silence in a room.

I give him a curt "thanks" just as the elevator dings its arrival on the first floor, just seconds before the doors open.

We both exit the elevator in silence and I turn left toward the mail boxes while Chuck heads straight through the lobby and out the front doors in a rush.

Upon seeing me, Betty calls from her chair requesting I come over when I am done with my mail.

I give Betty a wave and an "okay" and then place the bills into the chute marked "OUT".

Moving over to my box, I place the small key in the lock but the entire time my attention is behind me. I am listening for footsteps or any other sounds of someone sneaking up on me, watching the reflections in the boxes for movement. I quickly open the box, retrieve my mail, and lock it. Quickly turn around and look around. The foyer is still empty, save for Betty in her rocking chair. I let out a deep breath trying to beat back the fear wiggling its way back in.

With a final deep breath, I tuck my mail under my arm and head over to the elderly woman with a smile on my face. If I cannot control my emotions, the least I can do is mask them.

As I approach her chair, I place my hand on her shoulder and lean in placing a kiss on the top of her head and greet her warmly.

Betty smiles up at me before reaching down into the basket that sits beside her chair. She pulls out a black ball of knitted fabric and when I open it, I see it is a beautiful shawl.

As I am looking at it she proudly says "I made it for you dear, since I am unable to leave this old chair without too much pain. I just wish I could have gotten it to you while you were still in the hospital."

Holding it up I draw in a sharp breath, "It is beautiful" I whisper in both shock and awe.

Betty had patterned a set of angel wings into the shawl coming out from the center and ending at the points on either end So that it looked as if the wings were spread in flight.

"I thought my little angel needed a set of wings to protect her" Betty says proudly as I wrap the shawl around my shoulders holding the end against my chest.

I am speechless and end up just giving Betty a hug as silent tears streak my cheeks.

Betty apologizes again for not being able to visit me in the hospital but her age and arthritis makes it impossible for her to move around unassisted anymore, so she worked on that shawl for me instead.

Thanking her and hugging her again, I nearly drop my mail but it is worth it. I let her know that I completely understand and never thought poorly of her for not visiting. I know about her pains and would never want her to hurt herself on my account. With warmth in my heart, I give her another hug and then I hurry back up to my apartment, smiling the entire trip up in the elevator. After locking the locks, I pull the bathroom door closed so I can look at myself wearing the shawl in the full length mirror on the outside of the door. The shawl is magnificent and I decide I will wear it always when I am in the apartment so that I can feel the warmth and love it gives me and stave away the fear and anger.

Still smiling, I head into the living-room where I sit on the couch and turn on the television. Putting my feet up on the coffee table, I am immediately immersed in an old black and white Béla Lugosi film I found on A&E. I do not even notice the time flying by, until there is a knock on the door.

I call out "Who is it?"

Dean replies with "Would you believe Prince Charming?"

Laughing the entire way to the door, I check the peephole and then let him in.

He holds up a pizza box with a bag on top and offers it as a peace offering since he was an hour later than he told me he would be.

I let out a quick laugh and follow it with a kiss to his cheek. Quickly, I grab the bag and look inside.

"What's in the foil?" I ask as I head for the kitchen.

Dean tells me he hopes I like hot wings, to which I nod and set them on the table while asking if he got the locks on the door. Dean sets down the pizza and goes back to lock the door while I get out plates and napkins. When Dean returns, I already had plates out and served the pizza and was just about to serve the wings. He waits for me to grab mine and then he piles several onto his plate as well as the little tub of blue cheese. Pulling out a bottle of water from the fridge for Dean I hand it to him and then topped off my coffee mug. With mug in one hand I grab my plate and a pile of napkins with the other and head into the living-room. Dean had set up a wooden tray table for each of us to set our plates on, so we were able to sit down with our food and watch the rest of the movie. Dean was more focused on the food than the movie, but several times I find myself with my food perched just outside my mouth suspended in anticipation of what is about to happen in the film.

When Dean walks out to retrieve more pizza, I barely notice him move, completely engrossed in the film, and then again when he went to get the last of the wings just before the movie ends.

When it finished, Dean shuts off the television and asks about my day, including how my appointment went.

I tell him about my visit with the doctor first and ask about my paid bills, to which he had no clue. I then I tell him about my excursion down to get the mail and stand to show off my beautiful shawl. I raise my arms up and out holding it open across my back so he can have the full view of it.

Dean compliments it and tells me he thinks it is great I was able to go down on my own and that he is proud of me, giving me a supportive hug.

I ask about his day next and after he gives me the short version he reaches behind him to the chair. He pulls a couple movies from the inside pockets of his jacket and hands them to me. I look them over, shaking my head at the second choice and then heads over to the DVD player putting in the first one. I cuddle into him, shawl wrapped around me and we watch the movies late into the night and as before, and I tuck him in before heading to bed myself.

Chapter 5

I am jolted awake by a loud tapping sound. It is nearly pitch black in my room and my eyes take a few moments to adjust as I looking around frantically for the source. Looking down the end of the bed I see the outline of someone in the doorway of my bedroom.

At first I think it is Dean but as my eyes adjust more, I realize it is definitely not Dean, but instead it is the man… The man that took me and tortured me and left me lying in the cold, bleeding.

I watch in terror as his fingers tap on the door frame, frozen in fear. RAP TAP TAP RAP TAP TAP over and over.

I try to scream but no sound comes out and suddenly, I can feel the tape across my mouth. When I try to reach for it, I realize my arms are tied down and I am bound to the bed. Tugging against the ropes, I try to get free but am unable.

As I fight against the ropes he threatens me with "I'm back to finish what I started" bringing my attempts to a halt.

I watch in terror as he slowly walks toward the bed. His outline fading into the darkness as he moves away from the soft light from the hall and closer to me. The closer he gets, the more I smell something horridly coppery. As he moves through a beam of light from the crack between the curtains, I see he is covered in some sort of thick dark liquid that shimmers against his clothing. Flailing, I try to scream for Dean and pull tightly against the bonds ripping into my skin.

The figure stops and laughs that horrible laugh I had hoped to never hear again.

He tells me Dean is dead and that he was going to bathe me in his blood by the end of the night but not until he brings forth my own blood to mingle with it.

Tears course down my cheeks as he takes the last few steps to the bed and crawls onto it like an animal stalking its prey. I feel his weight on the bed shifting as he moves closer. I feel his hot breath against my bare skin and I try to move upward to get away from him but I am stopped by the headboard, smacking my head into it. Realizing I may have a way out I slam my head back hoping to bring on unconsciousness. The first attempt left my head swimming but was not enough.

Unfortunately, before I can do it a second time he grabs my ankle and pulls me down, climbing on top of me. His body is pressed down into mine and he reaches up and grabs my hair with his left hand, resting his elbow on the bed to prop himself up. His face is inches from my own as he caresses my cheek with his right hand leaving a smear of blood across it. Moving even closer he grips my face as if to give me a kiss but the tape saves me from the horror. He then licks the blood from my cheek and slides his hand down my neck and over my shoulder toward my breast, gripping it tightly.

I jolt awake with a bloodcurdling scream that startles Dean from his bed on the couch. I hear his quick steps down the hall before he throws the door open flipping the light on and rushing in. My eyes temporarily blinded by the sudden light panics me as he searches the dark for an intruder.

The room is empty but for me sitting upright in the middle of the bed, clutching my blankets to my chest and hyperventilating as I look around the room as well.

Realizing it was a nightmare, he calls my name trying to get me to acknowledge him before he approaches.

It takes several calls before I turn toward him, but it took a few moments for me to truly see him and realize he really is still alive. As soon as he sees the realization in my eyes, he rushes to me.

Taking me into his arms and cradling me against his bare muscular chest he whispers into my hair "it's okay, you are safe now, it's okay."

As a firefighter, Dean was trained to acknowledge shock victims as well as how to handle them, although he was obviously surprised seeing my previous night's progress. Dean holds me tight and continues to whisper into my ear letting me know I am safe and that he is here with me. As my shaking becomes less violent and my breathing slows, he loosens his grip on me, giving me a little room to move if I want to. When I do not pull away, he backs up a little and still holding my arms he asks if I am okay.

He's searching my face and eyes and when I do not respond, he asks if I want to talk about it. I tell him I would rather not and he suggests I talk to doctor Friedmann about it tomorrow then since I should really share it with someone.

I nod my head and give a soft "Okay" before cuddling back into his arms, hoping to chase away the chills still running through my body. After a short time, he asks if I want him to sleep in here the rest of the night. I hesitate before deciding to let him stay and then I asked him to leave the room while I put on my pajamas. I am not comfortable sleeping with him in the nude quite yet.

Dean leaves, promising to be just outside the door "only a call away." Closing the door most of the way, but leaving a small crack for comfort I can see his back to the door.

Cautiously walking to my dresser, I open the top drawer. Out of the corner of my vision I notice my reflection in the mirror and I see my image staring back at me with wide frightened eyes and pale cheeks.

Was this what a shock victim looks like, I wonder? Is what Dean saw on my face that first day Dean found me? Shaking my head to clear away those thoughts, I pull out my favorite pair of pajamas which are a matching short sleeve button up and pants set in dark purple fleece. I rub the fleece against my face both for the comfort of the soft fabric and to wipe away the residual ghostly feeling of his hand. After I finish dressing, I call Dean back in.

He enters the room with a smile and makes a wise-crack about how he liked my previous outfit better, giving me a wink to know he is playing around.

I give him a halfhearted glare and then point to the right side of the bed. "You sleep over there please" I tell him as I start to climb into the left side of the bed. "Oh and get the light too."

After turning off the light, Dean makes his way in darkness to the bed and after climbing in, attempts to cuddle me against him. I jump at his touch and I push him back onto his side, reminding him he is only there to sleep. I may need the comfort of his being close, but I cannot handle being touched in the dark after that nightmare, not so soon anyway.

He apologizes and tells me he was just trying to be comforting.

I explain why I jumped and he apologizes again before rolling over and soon falling asleep. I however, am unable to fall back to sleep so easily. At first, I lay there listening to Dean's heavy breathing, hoping he does not snore, but soon my thoughts lead to the dream. I can still feel his touch on my skin and see his eyes in the darkness staring down at me. The dream felt so real. As sleep starts to finally tickle at my conscious, I begin to imagine myself not as the victim but instead putting that evil man in my place. Forcing **him** to be afraid, and I find the idea comforting. Finally sleep comes as I dreams of revenge.

As the sun rises and my alarm, which I set for Dean, goes off, I wake groggily and find that a mixture of fear and revenge is still lingering in the corners of my thoughts. The dreams of seeking revenge, mingled with the nightmare, created a strange and frightening scenario in my mind. I am visibly shaken and the idea of leaving the house alone was even less appealing now. The trip to get the mail alone was difficult enough and although I managed it, it left me feeling worn out by the time I returned to my place. The alarm still going off pulled me from my thoughts and I give Dean a shove when he does not wake on his own. When he starts to get up, I turn the alarm off and get out of the bed. I let him hit the shower first while I start the coffee and then I get a quick one myself.

Dean had told me last night that he was going to be working again today so he would not be able to take me to the appointment, so over breakfast I hesitantly mention I am afraid to go alone. He tells me he wishes he could go with me but that he needs to go to this meeting and offers his best friend Anthony - or as he says it, Ant-knee - to escort me.

I hesitantly accept after he vouches for his friend and ensures me I will be safe with him. Dean then flips open his cell to call his friend, explaining the situation.

Anthony says he is more than happy to help out and he lets him know he will be there early so we can have a chance to get to know each other a little before we leave.

Dean thanks him and closing the phone he tells me he wishes he could be there the first time we meet but that he will just have to "deal with it."

Before putting his phone away Dean shows me the picture of Anthony he has as his contact ID image. It's difficult to see details but I notices he is very much the stereotypical young Italian male from this area with his dark hair and eyes, strong features and he is built just like Dean. The only difference between Anthony and every other Italian guy I've met in this area is his eyes.

Dean had mentioned Anthony's mother is Irish, and he had inherited his mother's blue green eyes. At least I know how to ensure it is him when he comes to the door. Dean also explains that Anthony knows to keep me safe and will take his role as escort and bodyguard quite seriously.

I cannot help but smile even though I am wrapping myself tightly in the shawl.

Dean points it out and asks if I am really going to be okay and offers to call in if I really need him.

I assure him I will be fine and we head into the living-room where he gives my some tips for lifting weights to distract me before he has to leave.

He told me if I am going to start lifting, I might as well start today. I think he just wanted the weights out when Anthony shows up so that it appears he's settling in my apartment, but I did not say anything.

I really like Dean and do not want to do anything to scare him off, especially since I am terrified of being alone.

After giving me a few pointers he kisses me on the top of the head and gets ready to go.

I walk him to the door and decide to give him my spare set of keys so that he can let himself in if I am not home when he gets out. It seems crazy after only really knowing him a couple days, but in those two days he has done more for me than anyone has my whole life. I see him off, only locking the door locks, leaving the chain unlatched and headed back into the living-room to work out until Anthony arrives. Facing the door so that I can see if someone tries to get in, I lift the weights, giving me something to preoccupy my mind while I waited.

About an hour before the appointment, there is a knock at the door. I peer through the peephole and see my new bodyguard, amazed at how vivid the color of his eyes really is.

I still ask "Who's there?" out of propriety and Anthony answers with "Ets me, Ant-knee."

I let him in and introduce myself.

He tells me Dean's told him a lot about me, which makes my blush and he chuckles.

I take the opportunity to ask him about Dean as we sit at the kitchen table drinking coffee. I thought it would be strange having a man I never met in my home but sitting and drinking coffee made it a little less uncomfortable. We continue to talk until about thirty minutes before my appointment. Anthony helps me rinse out the mugs before we leave the apartment and he drives me to the hospital. When we arrive, he parks in the side lot by the General Admissions entrance and walks me in.

In the main lobby he asks if I want him to go up with me or if I would be okay with him leaving and coming back after the appointment.

I decide to be strong and go up alone and he promises to return in an hour, offering to meet me back here in the lobby. I agree and he heads toward the double doors as I get onto the elevator.

He turns and gives me a thumbs-up as the elevator doors close. I cannot help but smile at the silly gesture as I ride up to the third floor. While waiting in Doctor Friedmann's waiting room, I glance through the assorted and extremely out-of-date magazines. Just as I decide on an old issue of Hot Rod magazine, I am called in.

After the initial niceties, the doctor sits in his executive rolling chair and I sit in a very comfortable overstuffed chair. I take a moment to look around his surprisingly sparse office with its solid oak desk and bookshelf full of what all appears to be psychological texts. There are no pictures on the walls, just his decoratively framed diplomas and certificates.

After settling in, I tell him about how I succeeded in getting the mail on my own without any severe issues, and that I even took the elevator. I share about the beautiful shawl and even show it to him since I thought I might need it on this trip out. I admit that coming here was nearly impossible without someone with me, since the idea of walking out there on my own was less than comforting.

He starts by congratulating me for succeeding in getting the mail on my own and then he tells me that it was okay for me to feel apprehensive about going outside alone. He suggests a self-defense class to build my self-reliance and I tell him Dean already plans to take me to his gym and get me enrolled in a class. The doctor tells me that it is the perfect place for taking a class and that Dean can even work out while I am in my class so that I will not have to go alone at first. I ask if it needs to be a self-defense class or if I can take something like Kick Boxing or Tai Chi and he tells me that would be acceptable since they are strength training classes but that a self-defense class would also assist in getting rid of my fears as well as give me insight into how to get out of an attack should it happen again. I make some notes in my little spiral bound notepad I keep in my jacket pocket and consider what he is telling me. Doctor Friedmann then tells me that he found out who was paying my bills while I was in the hospital; it was Officer Pacitti and the crew down at the 62nd Precinct.

I make a note to get down there with a big batch of fresh baked cookies and a carafe of fresh made coffee for them as a thank you.

The remainder of the visit is spent with the doctor giving me new tasks and more advice.

Originally, I was going to tell him about the nightmare but then decided to wait and see if it happens again before making a big deal of it. Besides, the dream has fueled that dark spot within me, the spot that stops me from being afraid and if I talk about it with the doctor, I may no longer have that spot to draw strength from.

I leave the office feeling a little better but it was not until I get down to the lobby and see Dean waiting for me that I feel a weight lift from my chest.

I practically run from the elevator and throw myself into his arms, asking "What are you doing here?"

He laughs and explains that Anthony's girlfriend had a fit about him helping "some other woman" so he called Dean and had to back out of picking me up.

He tells me that Anthony felt really bad and hopes there will be no hard feelings. I shake my head and let him know I am fine with it, more than fine.

As we walk out to the car, I ask if he is going to get into trouble at work for leaving early and he assures me that his boss remembers me and has no problem with him taking the rest of the day off to help me out. Smiling I tell him about the station paying my bills and my plan to bake cookies so he offers to take me to the store to get the supplies on the way home. I am so happy that I give him a big kiss on his cheek before I realize what I am doing. Before I have a chance to regret kissing him, he grabs my hand and leads me out to the car with a big grin on his face. It is a short drive to the store and Dean manages to get a spot right up front so I do not have to walk so far in the open lot. As we enter the store I grab a cart and we head to the baking aisle where I get a large bag of flour and a couple bags of chocolate chips. Next I grab a pound of Columbian coffee and run it through the grinder they have in the store. From there we head over to the refrigerated section to get some unsalted sweet cream butter, a carton of eggs, and a bottle of vanilla creamer.

Dean grabs some Doritos and a bottle of orange juice and we head to the check-out. We actually make it through the checkout without any magazines or candy and load the bags into the car.

When we get back to my apartment, I make up enough dough for four dozen chocolate chip cookies. I then recruit Dean's help in putting the dough on the cookie sheets and most of the afternoon is spent baking the several trays of cookies.

While we wait, Dean decides we should go lift weights and train some more. He wants to see if I remember what he showed me this morning but instead, I start off by trying to jump rope. After whipping myself in the calf several times due to the small area I have to work in I give up and go to the weights with Dean after all. He watches me as I do the moves he showed me, while he works on his arms some too.

He promises to take me to the gym first thing in the morning since the doctor was not going to be visiting until later in the afternoon, but for now he is showing me a few techniques to tide me over. He plans to introduce me to the owner of the gym and find out what they have to offer as far as classes.

Dean has never had an interest in the classes so he was unable to help me with information and the gym's website only states "contact us for a complete list of current classes."

We hear the timer ding in the kitchen and head back in to finish off the baking. As the last batch of cookies comes out of the oven, I start up a large pot of coffee to bring with the cookies to the precinct. Placing all the cookies into a large cookie tin I saved from the holidays a couple years back, I wrap them in some tissue paper to protect them. It is a very large blue circular tin with a large silver bow painted on the top, which I thought it was appropriate for them. Putting the coffee in my carafe, I hand it to Dean with a bag containing the creamer and rest of the ground coffee while I grab the cookies and we head out the door.

When we arrive and I hold up the tin of cookies and coffee, the officers are quite happy. We are escorted into the back and setting them on the break room table, I watch happily as they each take a handful of cookies and fill their mugs.

One of the officers, a short blonde woman, takes the bag of coffee and heads over to their coffee maker to start up a new pot since the carafe was nearly empty already and she didn't get a cup yet.

After Officer Pacitti finishes his cookies, I ask to speak with him in his office. We head back and I tell Pacitti I had a nightmare the previous night involving the man that attacked me and that it brought back memories of bits and pieces I saw of him. I remember that he had a crew cut and that his hair was a dark brown. He also had a small scar in the shape of a C just above his left ear.

He asks if I would be willing to look through their mug shots, and after getting a nod from Dean that he's fine waiting I agree.

I spend several hours looking through the men fitting the description but he is not there.

Pacitti tells me that it means the perpetrator has not been in the system yet, which troubles him even more. He thanks me for trying and escorts us back to the break room to retrieve my carafe before walking us out.

I am very disappointed, so Dean decides to take a side trip to the video store on the way back to my place.

He convinces me to not get anything that has too much blood or gore after what was obviously a reaction to the "Saw" movie we watched last night.

I point out to him that action movies would be out as well by those standards and Dean laughs at my call.

We eventually end up getting a comedy and a romance, neither of which I am too enthusiastic about, but it is a compromise we both agreed on.

Dean assures me he would make it up to me later if I am too disappointed, so I smile and after checking out we head back to my place for another movie night in.

When we get back to my apartment, Dean throws a frozen pizza into the oven for dinner while I set up the first movie, "Madea Goes to Jail."

Dean insisted that the Madea movies are hilarious and that I will like it but I was not so sure. How could a man dressed up as a loud, overbearing woman be funny.

About halfway through the movie I understand having spent nearly the entire time laughing so hard it hurt and I even managed to snarf some pizza out my nose which really hurt but sent Dean into a laughing fit so I punched him in the arm. I am finding it helps to take my mind off everything else as well; perhaps laughter **is** the best medicine. The second movie Dean puts in is "The Back-Up Plan" which throughout the entire movie I cannot wait for it to end. Suffering through it, I wonder why I let Dean talk me into renting it since I have never liked romance flicks but he appears to be enjoying it, so I do not say anything. An hour and forty four minutes later, I am rushing into the kitchen for the jar of Nutella and a package of whole wheat Ritz crackers just to escape being asked about the movie. I seriously need a treat after sitting through that movie.

"What on earth?" I exclaim as Dean walks in, catching me off guard. He laughs, apologies and offers to "make it up" to me.

I threaten to throw him out in the street if he ever makes me watch something like that again and tell him **nothing** could make up for that. He laughs again and gives me the Scout's Honor sign before going back into the living-room.

I hear music playing and realize he has put in another movie but cannot remember when he picked a third one up. Walking back into the room with the Nutella in one hand, crackers and knife in the other, I see him sitting on the couch reclining back and waiting.

When he sees me, he tells me to put the snacks down and come and cuddle. Giving him a sideways glance, I set things down on the coffee table before sitting on the couch.

When I look at the television I bursts into laughter because on the screen is "Mutant Vampire Zombies from the 'Hood!"

He tells me that he picked it up earlier as a surprise and I could not help but forgive him.

The movie was a really bad B-rated horror flick but I knew that and found myself giggling more than anything.

After watching the movie, I ask Dean if he will be joining my in the room again tonight.

When he confirms, I go into my room first and change into my pajamas while Dean changes into his flannel pants in the bathroom.

We then take turns brushing our teeth and I meet Dean in the bedroom. I am sitting at the foot of the bed, my head bowed down. Concerned, Dean sits next to me, taking my hand and asks what is bothering me. I tell him that I am still uncomfortable with him sleeping in my room since we have not been dating that long but that I really cannot sleep on my own right now.

He tells me he completely understands and that he promises to behave and not do anything that will make me uncomfortable.

With a heavy sigh, I get up and go to my side of the bed and he goes to his. Together we pull down the blankets and get into the bed, pulling them back up over us.

As we say goodnight, Dean rolls over and shuts the lamp off on his side of the bed, leaving us in darkness. I feel him move around and soon he falls asleep. I lay awake for quite a while trying to decide whether I am more uncomfortable with Dean in the bed or with the impending nightmares. Finally I drift to sleep after cuddling up to his back and wrapping my arm around him. I can feel his chest rise and fall with each breath and it is comforting. Listening to his heartbeat against my ear, I finally drift off to sleep.

Chapter 6

I give Dean a kiss on the cheek goodbye as he heads out the door to go to work. As with the previous day, I lock the two locks, leaving the chain dangling against the door in case he needs to get back in. I hop in the shower to shave and try out the deep conditioner I picked up on the way home in the hopes it will help with the mass of frizz forming on top my head. When I returned from the hospital, I cut my hair to shoulder length and dyed it a brownish red. I wanted a change and figured a change of identity might keep the evil man from recognizing me as quickly. Unfortunately, the store-bought boxed hair dye seems to have dried it out quite a bit, leaving it feeling like straw and extremely frizzy. Stripping down, I look in the mirror and the scars seem to be darker, fresher looking than they had this morning when I dressed to go to the gym. I decide to write it off as a side effect of the workout, seeing I got quite hot and sweaty. Turning the water on getting into the shower, I wash down with my favorite Key Lime scented body wash and then shave my legs. When I am done, I wash my hair with a color-extending shampoo and smooth in the three minute conditioner, read the directions after I am done applying it. I always forget to read first and luckily I applied it properly. Now to wait.

Since I do not have a clock in the shower, I turn the heat up a little and turn my back toward the water allowing it to flow over my body as I count one M-I-S-S-I-S-S-I-P-P-I, two M-I-S-S-I-S-S-I-P-P-I in my head.

It is silly I know, but I have used that method for years, ever since I learned it in elementary school. I reach one hundred and eighty and just as I am about to rinse my hair I hear the front door open. Figuring Dean forgot something, or that he decided to take the day off, I quickly finish rinsing my hair out. I am just about done when the bathroom door opens.

I am unable to see who is entering the bathroom through the design on the curtain so I call Dean's name and asks if everything is okay.

There is no answer, so I grab for my towel that I draped over the curtain rack, but is not there. I start to panic, calling Dean's name just as the curtain is thrown open and a large hand grabs me by the throat. I try to scream, but all that escapes is a gurgling sound. Frantically, I claw at his hand as I raise my head up and look into his face. Suddenly I remember everything from that day. I look into his face, the same face that looked up at me in the alley. His squared jaw with light stubble, his nearly black soulless eyes, the same eyes that peered at me over the mask in the building, the scar across the top of his crooked nose, and he looks at me with the same evil grin. I stop fighting and he loosens his grip slightly. This is his first mistake, and I rake at his face with my nails. He drops me, his hands going to his face. As he turns to look in the mirror, I scramble out of the tub. I nearly reach the door when he punches me in the side. As I fall onto the cold tile floor, he kicks me in the stomach, knocking the wind and fight out of me. This time however, I refuse to scream, I will not give him the pleasure. Instead, I look up at him with hatred in my eyes and he kneels down on one knee and smacks my across the cheek. Blood pools in my mouth from the cut that formed when my teeth penetrated the inside of my cheek and I spit it into his face. He smacks me again, harder this time and slams me down onto the floor. Gripping my shoulders, he forces himself between my legs.

He tells me that this time he will finish what he started and nothing will stop him this time.

As his left hand works at his pants, his right grips my throat again and he presses his thumb in the soft spot behind my jugular, threatening to pop it out. He works himself free and moves into position. I can feel him pressed against me. Just as he is about to penetrate me, I force myself awake, my hands flying up to cover my mouth and stifle the scream threatening to escape.

I quickly look over at Dean, who is sound asleep, snoring lightly. My heart is racing as I slowly move my hands from my mouth and try to catch my breath, being careful not to wake Dean. I remember him now and carefully I get out of bed and sneak into the living-room. There I take out my sketch pad and drawing pencils. I flip to a page three quarters of the way through the pad and on a blank page I draw the man's face. Closing my eyes occasionally so that I can capture every detail, I complete the image and then close the pad. Finally, I quietly put everything away and head back to bed. On the way back, I make a stop in the kitchen and pull out a glass. Heading to the refrigerator, I pour a small amount of juice into it and leave it on the counter. I then stop by the bathroom and flush the toilet in case Dean wakes as I am getting back in the bed. A drink and trip to the bathroom, perfect cover if necessary. As I carefully get back in the bed, I consider my options and decide to not give the sketch to the police because they cannot give that man the punishment he deserves. Instead, I will find him and teach him a lesson in suffering he will never forget. As I lay there trying to rid my thoughts of the nightmare, I imagine how I would punish him and the seed sprouts its sharp barbed shoot. Vividly, I remember the pain he caused me, and I intend to make him feel it all. An eye for an eye they always say. This time, I have no problem falling back asleep, the blanket of revenge comforting me, and my dreams are filled with it.

The following morning Dean, and I get up early to get ready for the gym. I put on a pair of navy blue Yoga pants with a light gray stripe down the sides and a light gray tank top with my navy blue sports bra underneath it. I finish off the outfit with my black Chucks, iPod armband and pull my hair back with a headband. Dean sports a pair of black sweats, a tight fitting white muscle shirt and a pair of white Nikes. Looking him over, I cannot help but see how hot he looks and wonder if I will be fighting women off at the gym. He grabs the gym bag he packed for us and takes my hand and we head out.

It is a short drive and when we arrive, I am not impressed by the exterior. It's red and white façade looks worn and outdated but when we walk in I am amazed by the place. The equipment is neatly arranged everywhere and at the back, behind floor to ceiling glass walls, are the classrooms. We walk around the outer edge of the room on the path and past the rooms which are large and clean, which impresses me.

When we reach the office in the back right corner, I talk with the owner Jimmy, whom Dean is good friends with, and he sets me up in the kick-boxing class that meets on Mondays, Wednesdays, and Fridays at 6am. Tuesdays and Thursdays, I can work on weights and Cardio if I want.

Since they are nearing the end of the current class track, Jimmy offers to give me a little personal training for the rest of the week as a favor to Dean. As he speaks with me, I cannot help but notice his overly muscular build that contrasts greatly with the soft features of his face. I wonder if Jimmy was picked on a lot as a kid and if that is what led him to becoming a muscular monster.

When he is done talking, he gives me the layout of the gym and then takes me over to the treadmill. After pushing some of the buttons, he tells me to get on.

When I do, he hits the start and I am in motion. I am told to run for twenty minutes and he says that he will be back when I am nearing the end of the time, to bring me to my next challenge.

I thank him and as he walks, away I pull the ear-buds from my armband, plug them into my ears and turn on my iPod. "Basketcase" by Greenday starts blasting inside my head. I move to the song, thinking it ironic it was the first one to play when I hit shuffle, but then it was followed by "The Becoming" by Nine Inch Nails and "Forgive Me" by Godsmack. I was beginning to wonder if someone was messing with my music when "Tubthumping" by Chumbawamba starts playing and I could not help but giggle.

Jimmy comes up just as the next song was starting to play, so I hit pause and pull out one of the buds so I can hear him.

He asks me what I hope to accomplish and I tell him I want to be able to protect myself without becoming overly muscular and losing what little feminine form I have.

He laughs and brings me over to the free-weights and puts me on something called a curl machine that will work my arm muscles.

He shows me three different moves on it and telling me to get to and that he will return in a bit.

Popping my bud back in and hitting play, Linkin Park starts to fill my head and I begin working on my biceps first. After being at the gym for an hour, I am exhausted and ready to go home. Looking around, I find Dean lifting weights along the side wall near the back, and Jimmy is with him. I walk up to them and tell them I am done.

Jimmy give me a "You did well for your first time" and gives Dean a pat on the back before he walks off to help someone else.

Dean gives me a big grin, looking at the sweat on my face. Handing me a towel, he asks if I want a shower first.

I look horrified at him and tell him I can wait until I get home and he asks if he could come home and join me.

I give him a hard punch to his chest and he replies with "Take that as a no" and then laughs as he gets up.

He tells me that he wants to grab a shower, and I decide to head out on my own.

I tell him about this class the YMCA is offering and how I want to go and sign up for it as per the doctor's suggestion.

He tells me he needs to run a few errands and hit his place for more clothes anyway and asks me to give him a call after my appointment and I get home.

With a kiss, I head out and walk the five blocks to the Y, constantly checking behind me nervously. The pamphlet states that the class is for women who have been physically or mentally abused and it offers both instructions on escaping an attack, as well as a support group with other women who have been in the same situation. The class itself seems like it will be informative and useful, but I wasn't sure I wanted to take advantage of the meetings. Had there been a way to avoid the gatherings, I would but it is a requirement for taking the course for free.

Looking over the pamphlet, I see the first thing they teach us in class is to overcome "the freeze response" which is what most women do when they are grabbed. Once we learn to control this, we will move on to physical protection, which is what I am more interested in.

As I sign up, they have me step in on one of the counseling groups currently meeting, to introduce myself. I sit down for a little while to see what it is all about. As I listen to these women tell their stories, I feel something inside me shift, this need to protect growing. As I listen to these women talk about their attacks and how they feel helpless, I want to fight for them. Suddenly the idea sparks what if I *could* fight for them? What if I were to become a guardian angel of sorts, one that exacts revenge on those evils? We are not alone, we have all been hurt and now I want to help stop others from being hurt as well. Between my self-defense lessons at the Y and the kickboxing class at the gym, I will be both stronger and more aware. As I listen to their pleas, something inside me grows stronger and stronger, giving me a purpose. I know why I survived now!

After leaving the YMCA, I decide to stop at the Mega-Mart near my place and pick up a small fire and waterproof security lockbox so that I have a safe place to store the sketch and anything else that may come up. When I get home, I place the key on a charm bracelet with a heart with a keyhole shaped cut-out in it, a pair of angel wings, a dove and a paintbrush, bits I bought in their craft department. The key is camouflaged perfectly on the bracelet hidden in plain sight and the bracelet will never leave my wrist. After some thought, I decide to hide the box in the bathroom, under the sink, where it was less likely to be found. Sitting on the floor, I loosen nine of the tiles in the shape of a square on the back wall under the cabinet with a screwdriver. Carefully, I scrape away the brittle caulk between the tiles and they easily pop out. I take them into the kitchen and carefully attach them to a piece of foam board from my craft supplies and add support braces on the back before leaving it to dry. Returning to the bathroom, I cut out the backer board from the wall where the tiles were and reveal a perfect sized opening for the box. Luckily, the floor spans between the rooms within the wall, and the braces are spaced just far enough apart for the box to fit between them. I leave the box in place and head back into the kitchen to check if the quick-dry glue worked, and it has. Carefully, I bring the faux wall back into the bathroom, trying not to fold it too much since it is still weak without the caulk. I slide the supports up on the top behind the wall and then carefully push the bottom in place. It is a snug fit, but it looks good. Satisfied with the fit I pull the piece back out and add the grout between the tiles to finalize the appearance. Pulling the box back out, I retrieve the sketch of the man.

Turning it over I write on the back *"Have you ever been hurt so bad by someone you wish you were dead? Or perhaps your pain was so deep you wished they were dead? I have known pain like this and I will do something about it. Hurt no more, fear no more, cry no more. Revenge is sweet and it is mine!"*

I place it in the box with a smile. It is this piece of paper and the words on the back that will encourage me to continue to move forward in my plans, and thus my true transformation begins. Tucking the box away I notice I still have at least an hour before my appointment, so I decide to begin my research.

Pulling out my laptop, I search for news articles on my abduction, looking for information on where I was taken in the hopes it will help me figure out where to find the man that took me. I know that the police are also looking for him, but they do not have his picture so they will not find him before I do. I come across an article GOWANUS BAY BUTCHERING with a byline of 'Young Woman Survives Brutal Attack!" It shows a picture of the building with the remains of the fire in front of it. I zoom in on the image after noticing a number on the building and write it down on a scrap piece of paper. I then print the article with the cover story of creating a healing scrapbook. Again, hiding the truth in plain sight. The Healing Scrapbook was an idea one of the ladies at the YMCA support group came up with in order to cope with what happened without burying it. Confront your fears and they cannot hold power over you. Story in place, article and address in hand, I head down to the docks in search of answers. Wandering around the dockyard, I am not sure I am going to be able to find the building at first as it is tucked among several others and the numbers do not appear to be in any particular order. When I finally find it, it becomes clear why he was so frustrated and had to end before he was finished. The area was still in use and he needed to finish before the workers started arriving in the early morning. I thought it was silly of him to work in such a public place and mentally noted that if I ever did seek revenge, I would want to pick someplace more secluded. Finally, I find the building in an obscure area, an abandoned warehouse tucked between an active warehouse and a dock office of some kind. Out front, all remains of the fire had been cleared away but there is still a large charred patch in front of the door that marks where it was. Old police line tape flaps from one side of the doorway and even though there are people moving in and out of the other buildings, nobody stirs in this one. I try to look through one of the windows but they have all been painted over since the incident.

As I move toward the next set of windows, a scruffy voice yells "HEY, you get away from those windows damn punk" and he stops suddenly when he realizes who he is yelling at.

He had been one of the first workers on site that horrible morning and watched them roll me out; I remember seeing the pity in his face. The same pity he has on it now as he stares at me in shock and wonder.

He continues to approach me and asks why I am here.

I tell him I want to see the place where I was tortured as part of my recovery process; my doctor wants me to face the demons of my past and see that they can no longer hurt me.

He buys the tale and offers to let me inside.

After a few moments of battling with my fears, I accept and the weathered old man lets me in. I walk through the door and over to the area that was still taped off although the tape is faded on the side facing the windows.

As he turns to leave, I ask when the windows were painted and he tells me it was done the day after the police were finished in there to keep the gawkers away.

He stands in the doorway for a few moments longer and then excuses himself, instructing me to call him when I am ready to leave so he can lock the place back up.

I thank him again and as he heads off, I turn to face my demons. The chain I was suspended from still hangs from the ceiling and there are stains on the ground beneath it. Walking up to the spot, I kneel down and touch it. Dry and cold. Shaking my head to ward off the frightened thoughts, I pull my travel sketch pad out of the messenger bag on my side and start drawing the scene from different angles. I end with the one I viewed from my position on the chain. I make sure not to miss any minute detail, as they could all be important. Being in the cold musty building, I begin to have flashbacks; a long shock session, the small slices on my sides, the way he caressed my face, those dead eyes. I make notes and draw sketches of everything I remember and after what feels like several hours,

I head out to let the dockhand know I am leaving.

He wishes me well and watches me leave, hoping the visit helped heal some of the pain I must have endured.

I thank him and tell him it did, even though in my mind, I only see my suffering and how I will make that pain go away. The pain will end, when the evil man's pain begins. Heading home, my mind is reeling with memories and ideas, building as I tuck my notes away and continuing all the way to Friedmann's office.

Before going in, I give Dean a call and ask if he would be willing to pick me up in an hour at the doctor's office since I would rather not travel home alone.

He more than happily agrees and I head in to tell the doctor what I have been up to, leaving out my true intentions.

After my appointment, I head down to the lobby to find Dean waiting.

He gives me a hug and asks if I am okay, since he heard a hint of something in my voice earlier.

I tell him about my day and he gives me a big hug. As we get in his car, I smell Chinese and look in the back seat where he has a couple bags of food and another bag with movies in it.

"Hope you don't mind" he says as he nods back.

I tell him I don't mind at all, and thank him for thinking ahead because I had not. I let out a little laugh and touch his arm, thanking him again.

After we get back to my apartment, we eat and cuddle together to watch the movies before heading to bed. For the first time, I sleep without dreams.

Chapter 7

At each of my appointments with Doctor Friedmann, he tells me I am showing great progress and that he feels I am "coming along nicely." He is impressed with my eagerness to transform myself from being a victim to someone in control of my life.

I play the perfect patient, telling him everything he expects to hear, playing him into believing I have healed and moved on with my life. When I am on my own however, I can feel the desire for revenge burning inside, so I make plans.

Each night before Dean comes to visit and on the nights when he is not visiting; I pull out the sketch and feel the flames growing. What that man did to me was beyond horrific and the police have still not been able to find him, but then I never gave them the sketch either. I know he is out there and I am the only one that knows what he looks like, so it will be up to me to stop him. Occasionally, I can feel him out there somewhere seeking his next victim and my hatred grows within my soul like an undetected cancer. I want him to feel the pain he inflicted upon me, I want him to scream and beg for mercy as I refuse to give it to him just as he had with me. I will not share these desires with anyone though, because I am afraid if I do they will "cure" me of it and that they will take away my ability to exact my revenge. On the nights that Dean cannot visit, I take time to watch the rapist I am tracking as well, which brings me a sense of peace that I carry to the appointments. As I reach the doctor's two-week marker with flying colors, he allows me to return to work. And so my new routine begins as does my first step toward balancing normality and my secret life. Every morning, I either go to the YMCA for a class or to the gym for a workout and every night I dress, tuck my can of mace into my pocket and head to work or to watch the rapist. I walk that same path, only now all the lights work and in the distance I see a police car patrolling the neighborhood.

On my first night back to work, I go downstairs and there Betty tells me they fixed them after my attack and I was angry it took someone getting hurt for them to finally do it, but glad it is finally done. Betty is a feisty little old woman and I imagine she had quite a bit to say to the powers-that-be about the subject.

Officer Pacitti had also told me the car in fact did belong to a pimp and was not used in my abduction. The man was arrested for human trafficking and prostitution and the car was impounded.

The neighborhood has been cleaned up and I was safe to walk to work now. Even the homeless are no longer found in the alleys and I wonder what happened to them, hoping they were given help and not just thrown in jail for loitering or something like that. Feeling guilty, I make a mental note to ask about it.

My first night back to work is longer than usual, as I am somewhat of a celebrity. Everyone wanting to ask me questions and one man actually has the nerve to ask to see my scars.

At this point, my boss walks up and tells the man he has to leave and then he makes a general announcement that this is a bar not the set of Heraldo and that if they are going to continue to harass his staff, he will be forced to raise the price of drinks.

That stops the questions. I work the rest of my shift behind the scenes and head home to another movie night with Dean. It has been several days since we last saw each other with his training and my working, and I arrive home to find him waiting outside my door with a couple movies in one hand and an overnight bag in the other.

When I walk up to him, I cannot help but smile and give him a kiss before unlocking the door and asking why he did not just let himself in.

He explains how he did not want to frighten me by being in the house when I arrived home without letting me know first and that he did not want to bother me at work, so he waited outside.

As he sets the things in his hands down on the table, he looks at my grim expression and pulls me in for a kiss. After the kiss, I fall into him and cry silently.

When I regain my composure, I tell him about my horrible night at work. Dean picks me up, carries me into the living-room and sets me on the couch. He takes off my coat and boots and heads out to the hall where he locks up the door, retrieves the movies, dropping his bag inside my bedroom door on his way by. He then goes in, puts in a movie, and we cuddle together on the couch where we eventually fall asleep watching movies.

I take a couple of days off before I return to work. I finish off another long shift at the tavern and am glad for closing time. Locking the front door, I wave through the large smoke stained window at my boss. As I wave, I notice the muscle on my arm in my reflection. I cannot help but smile at the fact that I went from a ninety pound thin rail, to a one hundred twenty pound muscular woman in a couple weeks. I never thought that I could do it, but now as I look at my reflection, I feel a strong sense of accomplishment. It has been a long night at the bar and I am happy to be going home, I even find the light skip in my step that I thought was lost.

As I head home, I pass one of several alleys along my way and hear a scream cut short. It sounds like it came from the end behind the buildings. My first instinct is to run for help, but after what I went through, I know that every second counts and by the time help will arrive, she could be gone. Quickly and quietly, I make my way down the alley in the direction of the scream and when I reach the end of the building, I carefully look to the left and then to the right. There I see a woman being held up against a wall by a man twice her size. He has one hand over her mouth, pressing her head into the wall, and the other hand holds a pocketknife pressed into her ribs, just below her left breast. I can see the man whispering something into the woman's ear and suddenly her eyes go wide.

I know I am not ready to take the man down on my own, even with all the muscle I have now, so I yell "Freeze! NYPD!"

The man throws the knife and takes off around the opposite end of the building.

After a brief stop to check on the woman and retrieve the knife, I tell her to go for help.

Heading in the same direction he went, I search for him and it does not take long for me to find and catch up with him. I follow him from a distance until eventually he goes into an abandoned house several blocks away. I sit outside the building for a while and eventually he emerges looking all around, and when he sees it is clear, he slinks off. I follow him to one of the local low-income complexes and make a note of which building he goes to and what apartment he goes in. Luckily, it is a motel-style complex where all the stairs and walkways are outside, and the doors are all visible. I contemplate calling the police from the corner payphone and then I decide to go home instead. At my apartment, I write down everything I remember, as well as draw a sketch of the man. At first, I reconsider and pick up the phone to call Pacitti, but then I have another thought. I remembered hearing on the news that there have been several rapes around the area, and I believe one of the new ladies at the support group described that exact man at one of the meetings. I decide to go to my laptop and look into it before deciding whether or not to call. Sure enough, the description of the rapist in the news article fits the man I followed tonight. One of the articles even shows an inmate photo of him saying he was recently released for similar crimes. They **had** him and let him go and now he is hurting more women! With this revelation, I decide the police are incapable of doing their job properly and even if they do catch him, he will not receive adequate punishment since they let him go once already. This man has been wandering around in public, how could they not have captured him again by now if they were actually trying. Irritated with the thought of this, I decide to take matters into my own hands... but how? After some thought I make plans to do a little research but know better than to do it from my own computer. It is too late to go to the library tonight since it is near closing time and Dean will be over soon, so I decide to go in the morning after the gym.

Dean and I head to the gym at six in the morning so that he will have time to hit the showers and dress for work. After our workout, I give him a quick peck goodbye and head home for my shower and to prepare. I figure I have time since the earliest any of the libraries in the area opens at nine, so I grab a quick breakfast as well. After putting my notebook and pen in my bag, I head out to the library across town instead of the one close to home. Once there, I stand near the computers at one of the book shelves, pretending to be interested in the books but I am actually watching the people sitting at the computers, waiting for someone to sit down and log in. Eventually someone does and I make note of the number they enter. It was so easy, and I make sure to hold on to it for future reference. I then move further away from the computers down the aisle and sit pretending to read a book until she logs out and leaves. Quickly, I sit at the same computer, and log back in with the woman's card number. By using the same computer it would just look as if she lost connection or forgot something, which happens a lot. Once logged in, I start scouring the web for inspiration.

I go to a search engine, typing in 'safe torture' and come across many websites. I am amazed at the amount of content on the subject and even more amazed to find there are many clubs for something called BDSM in this area. I make notes of a couple of the addresses, as well as some of the information I see repeated on many of the sites. I am not able to get to the websites with images because the library blocks them due to 'violent content' or 'adult content' so I decide I will have to wander by one of the clubs and see for myself. After surfing the web a little longer, I decide to look up articles on the rapist again. I also search for images of the victims and print everything up, tucking them into my bag.

 As I leave the library, I decide I will need a couple things to pull this off without being recognized. After stopping at the apartment to stash my notes and print-outs, I head out on a road trip. Not having a car, and not wanting to have a paper trail by using a taxi, I decide to ask Betty if I can borrow her car. I tell her I need to run around a bit and do not want to pay the taxi fees.

Since Betty has lent me the old Buick before, she did not even question it. Fishing out the keys from her basket of yarn, she hands them over to me and tells me to drive safe.

Thanking her, I head out the back door to the parking lot and drive out of the city. The first place I hit is the Party City in Whitehall, PA which is a nearly two hour drive but I want to be sure to go far enough away so I will not run into anyone who may know me. I go in pick out a blonde wig in a bob cut first, trying it on to see how it looks. My hair sticks out a little and I look around for one of those caps you put your hair in before putting on a wig. After I find one, I place them both into my basket and head over to the costumes. I look at the wall of costumes and after deciding they will look too cheesy, I just gather ideas from the Goth themed ones and then I head to the check-out. On my way to the front of the store, I pass the shoes and see a pair of black over the knee pleather boots with a six inch heel on them. I try on a pair and am amazed at the height difference. Seeing they are on clearance, I decide to buy them as well.

Paying for the supplies with cash, I then head over to a plaza I remembered passing down the street. The plaza has assorted clothing shops spread throughout it and after going to four different ones, I manage to put together the perfect outfit. I walk back to the car, pleased that in my bags, I have the outfit I need for going undercover. The last thing I will need is some make-up, so I head to the drug store on the corner and find the make-up section. Grabbing a package of shadow in shades of purples and blacks, some liquid black eye liner and deep burgundy lip liner with matching lipstick, I head to the checkout. Before returning to the car, I make a stop at Staples and buy a package of rubber bands and a couple more composition notebooks for my notes.

When I get back to my place I excitedly try on the outfit. Looking in the mirror, I do not even recognize myself. On my feet are the new boots, my legs are hugged by a pair of black stressed jeans with interesting worn spots and holes in them. Under the jeans is a pair of deep purple tights, the color peeking through the worn spots. The jeans are low on my hips, and the top I picked shows off a good amount of my well-defined torso and belly button. As I look at the top I am glad to see it hides the padding in the bra that puts me from an A cup to a C cup, boosting my breasts up and filling the black corset nicely. Since it was sleeveless, I picked up a pair of long black sateen gloves that go three quarters the way up my arms. They serve two functions; first they hide my tattoo on my left wrist of a Blue Morpho Butterfly and second, they hide the blue Nitrile gloves beneath them. The biggest change however is when I reach my head. With my hair tucked properly in the cap, the wig looks almost natural and in the dim light of night and I hope it will not be noticeably fake. I chose a top of the line wig because out of the selection it was the closest to realistic I could find, but I made a note to go to an actual wig shop at some point to get a real one before my next job. It had taken my quite a while to get the wig secured well enough so that when I shake my head, it does not shift but it is worth it if it keeps me from being recognized. I then use the image on the package of eye shadow to do my make-up and the purple and blacks around my eyes mixed with the deep color on my lips make me look dark and depressed.

Turning, I check myself out one last time before deciding to test out my new look. Taking all the packaging from my purchases as well as the bags, I head to the incinerator chute and drop them in before heading downstairs. It is late enough at night that all of my neighbors are either in bed or at a bar somewhere, so I make it out of the apartment building without being noticed.

With the address of the first club in hand, I take a deep breath and start heading toward the trains. I made sure not to carry a purse, tucking my cash into my bra. I also have my can of mace secured down between my breasts, just in case. Luckily, the car I boarded was empty, so I sit on one of the seats that face the center of the train, giving me a view of both sets of doors. When I near my stop, I head toward a set of doors but seeing there is a homeless person on the far end of the tracks, I decide to take the exit closer to my side of the train even though it means walking an extra block on the street.

When I arrive at the club's address, I wonder if I wrote it down wrong. There is no sign, just a solid medal door painted black in the side of a brick wall with a strange symbol made out of steel on it. I turn to walk away when man opens the door and looks me over.

He asks if I am lost, and I tell him I am looking for the club.

He tells me I found it and then asks "Dom or Sub?"

I explain that I am unsure because this is my first experience with this particular lifestyle. I mention that I overheard some of my girlfriends talking about it and just had to look into it myself.

He shakes his head, laughing, and tells me I should not be here alone because even though they regulate the place, occasionally the newbies are taken advantage of but that he can hook me up with one of his people for tonight.

The man motions me inside the door where I can hear music coming up the steps and after closing the door behind me, he turns to make a call downstairs. I take the time to look him over. He seems normal enough, wearing tight black jeans, a black well-fitting tee shirt over his well-muscled body and a pair of black combat boots. He's in the typical bouncer uniform except for the multiple piercings. His hair is cropped short against his head like a fine auburn down and I have an overwhelming urge to touch it, but know better. When he turns back, I quickly avert my eyes.

He tells me that Druitt is on her way up and will be my escort for the evening but before I have a chance to ask who Druitt is, I see her coming up the stairs.

Gliding toward us comes a very tall, well-built woman wearing nothing but some leather straps strategically placed and thigh high spiked heel leather boots. She is also carrying a frightening looking object in her right hand, and her left slides up the banister. She has long wavy black hair sweeping down her back and curling around her ample breasts. Darkly tanned skin and deep brown eyes complete the Amazonian look. I have a moment to doubt the plan before Druitt smiles a large friendly smile and takes my hand.

"Hi love, I'm Druitt. Goodness you look terrified!" she exclaims as she laughs. "Don't ya worry, I will keep you safe" she assures me.

She sees me staring wide eyed at the thing in her hand she explains to me that it is a flail and not really as scary as it looks.

Handing it to me I move it around and give my wrist a snap, jumping when the leather straps snap back and gets my hand.

Giving it back to her, I shake my head and give a little "Ow."

She giggles and tells me I did it wrong but that she is sure someone in one of the rooms will be using one, so I will get a chance to see it in action.

As if that is her cue, she escorts me down the stairs into the darkened music-filled depths. My mind goes into overdrive as thoughts of people hanging from chains or chained to the walls like a dungeon fill it. When we reach the bottom however, I am greeted by what looks like a normal night club. There is a large dance floor with occasional cages and poles, but many of the dance clubs in the area have the similar décor. The only difference is there are both women and men inside the cages and instead of dancing on the poles, they are cuffed to them. On one pole, a woman is tied facing it, her feet are free and she is bent forward. Behind her another woman is using what looks like a canoe paddle with a much shorter handle to redden the first woman's exposed buttocks. Each time she makes contact there is a loud smacking sound and the receiver makes a noise of both pleasure and pain.

Druitt is watching my face and asks "Girl, I never even asked your name?"

I had read that people at these clubs generally do not use their given names but instead have club names so I say "You can call me Reaper."

Druitt laughs telling me I look too timid to be a reaper but then the quiet ones are usually the most dangerous. With that she asks what I might be interested in.

When I tell her I am trying to figure that out, she decides to give me the full tour of all the rooms.

After seeing everything the club has to offer, I let out a sigh of relief. There was no mutilation or blood anywhere and most of what was going on was within my limits of acceptance. Luckily, I have an open mind though, because some of the things I saw were highly sexual and left me a little uncomfortable.

Druitt asks if I know whether I am a Sub or a Dom and explains the roles of both.

I know immediately that I am a Dom. I explain that I have been on the receiving end and it just did not do it for me.

Druitt smiles and tells me that she would gladly help me find my niche, asking if anything in particular caught my attention.

I ask if we can return to the room with the woman using the little box.

Druitt giggles "Oh the nipple stimulator, that's so much fun" and escorts me back to the room decorated in deep burgundy and black.

Lying back on a pile of oversized pillows is a petite woman with short spiked hair. In the dim light, I cannot make out the color of it, but it appears to be blue.

As we walk back into the room, the woman on the pillows smiles broadly and asks Druitt if she is there to play with her.

Druitt tells her that they have a newbie in their presence, that I am interested in trying it out. I am surprised by this, as I thought I was just going to watch, not actually participate but I do not voice my thoughts.

The petite woman smiles broadly at me and introduces herself as Damselfish, or Dame for short, which makes me decide the hair is blue.

I introduce myself as I did with Druitt and she bows her head and holds out the box with both hands, head lowered.

Druitt tells me that Dame is giving me both dominance and request to use the stimulator on her.

Taking the box from Dame, I look to Druitt for instruction. She starts with a lesson in safely using the equipment. She points to where I attach things and after demonstrating on my pinky finger and then instructs me to attach it to Dame, who is waiting with obvious anticipation.

Having never touched a woman before, I was unsure if I would be able to do it, but Dame's pleading and Druitt's encouragement gave me no choice. I would be too embarrassed to show discomfort when Dame was being so trustful. Dame writhes under my touch with little sounds of excitement as I clip the ends in place and Druitt shows me how to play with the little knobs on the box and vary the stimulation to Dame. By the time the lesson is finished, Dame is lying back with a content grin on her face and I thank her for allowing me to learn with her.

She just lies back with a large grin and Druitt and I move on to several of the other rooms she thinks I may be interested in. For the rest of the evening, I followed Druitt as she teaches me different things and at the end, I am invited to return the following week for more extensive lessons.

On my way out, I inquire into where I can pick up some of the "toys" I learned to use tonight and Druitt gives me a card to a place just down the street.

With a smile, I tuck the card into my jeans and head home. The whole way, I put to memory what I learned and as soon as I walk into the apartment, I pull out my notebook and make notes on every little detail. I also make sketches of how things attached, and where, so I was sure not to forget a single detail. I intend to use this knowledge when I finally get a hold of the man that hurt me, but first I will practice on that rapist and maybe even a second criminal. After I finish making my notes, I tuck the book back into its home and decide to head out to the place I followed the rapist and see if he is around.

Tucking several sheets of folded paper and a pen into my jacket pocket, I walk to the site and from across, the street I check it out. There are lights on and I see movement in the abandoned building, so I head across and peek in. Once I confirm it is him, I keep to the shadows for the rest of the night, watching his movements and making notes of where he is and when. I note that he likes to drink a lot, which will help with my plans. It appears that he is the only person that uses this building but I will be sure to watch a few more times before committing to that thought. I do not want to get caught off guard the night I attempt to instill my punishment on him. At one point in the evening, he sits down to smoke a tightly-wound joint, which I can smell from my hiding place near the window. Between the large amounts of alcohol and cheap weed, he passes out so I decide to take the time to case the place. I walk around the building, making notes of each side of it and specifying each entry and exit point, as well as possible emergency exits. I make notes of which are easier and which are more hidden. When I am done, I head back to the room he is in and notice he is starting to stir, so I hide back outside and watch as groggily he hides his new knife behind a lose piece of molding on one of the walls. Quickly, I jot this down as it will be very important to know later on. He shuts off the LED lantern he is using for light and hides that as well and I follow him back to his apartment just before dawn.

When I get back to my apartment for the night, I change out of the outfit and try to figure out how to tuck them into the space in the bathroom wall without damaging anything. Reaching in the hole, I realize that the opening goes up further so I go out into the kitchen and remove one of the coffee mug hooks I never use because of their awkward placement from the cabinet and go back into the bathroom. Lying on the floor, I put the hook up on one of the beams by reaching my arm way in; this allows me to hang the bag with my carefully folded outfit in it, up out of site. Once everything is tucked, away and I write down my notes from the stake-out in my notebook and tuck it all away as well, I then decide to take a shower and remove any trace smells that might still be on me from my trips tonight. It takes several tries to get all the make-up off and I make a mental note to pick up some of that remover stuff I saw on the shelf next to the liners at the drug store.

When I get out of the shower, I take a quick glance at the clock and seeing that it is a little before five in the morning. I panic. I am supposed to be meeting Dean at the gym in an hour and a half but I am exhausted from the evening, as well as the long day before and just want to go to sleep. I know that if I do this however, without calling Dean, he will worry and possibly even just stop by so I decide to come up with an excuse that will both get me out of going and keep Dean from coming over to visit. Knowing Dean will be awake at this time, I pick up the phone and dial his number. After several rings he picks up and I wonder if he was asleep after all.

I hear him fumble with the phone and then when he gets on he apologizes and explains he was in the shower.

I feel bad for interrupting his shower and apologize and then tell him that I have been up all night with some sort of stomach thing. When he offers to come over and take care of me, I tell him I am just absolutely exhausted from spending the night in the bathroom and now that my stomach has settled, I just want to go to sleep.

He tells me he understands and wishes my better health soon and then we say our goodbyes and hang up.

Guilt nags at me, but I need to keep my secret and I truly do need the sleep. If Dean were ever to find out, he will try and stop me, or worse he might turn me in. He is a "good boy" right to the bone, and would not understand that what I am planning is indeed justice. I begin to wonder if things with him will continue to work, but cast them aside as I prepare for bed and drift off to sleep planning.

Chapter 8

I wake a little before noon and guilt still nags at me for blowing off Dean with a lie, so I decide to call him and ask if he wants to get together for lunch.

He is at work and needs to go to one of the other rooms before asking how I am feeling.

My stomach clenches and I tell him it was probably the jalapeno poppers I ate for dinner, because I am feeling fine now.

After a good scolding, he offers to pick me up in half an hour for a light lunch or something.

I tell him that sounds great and that I can't wait to see him. After I hang up and take a really quick shower and brush my teeth, I put on one of my favorite sundresses and a pair of sandals. The dress is a simple long one with an empire waist in navy blue and the best part is it has pockets for me to tuck things in. I am just about to head down to return Betty's keys, when Dean knocks at the door. After peeking through the peep hole, seeing it is him, I open it and he gives me a gentle hug. I cannot help but smile at him and give him a quick peck on the cheek. Suddenly, I lean into him for comfort for a moment. Quickly, I back up and grab my wallet, tucking it in my left pocket, and keys from the table right next to the door, I step out beside him and lock up, putting the keys in my right pocket. Taking Deans hand, we head down to the lobby.

In the elevator, Dean tells me he decided to go to this little bistro not far from my place since they offer light meals as well as burgers and such.

I give his arm a squeeze and thank him for thinking about me. On our way through the lobby, I notice Betty has nodded off in her chair so I decide to hold on to the keys a little longer. We decide to walk to the restaurant after a long debate over my health, and me winning. Still holding hands, we stroll down the street in a comfortable silence. I take the time to ponder our relationship and I feel bad for having to blow him off. I know I will have to do it again but I also know that he's burrowed his way into my heart. Any thoughts I may have had about leaving him flew out the door when I saw him standing there with that worried expression on his face this morning. As we arrive at the restaurant and sit for lunch we have the usual conversations about work.

Dean talks about a big fire he recently put out and how he saved a three year old girl from a third floor apartment.

I talk about this group of teenagers with fake ID's that tried to get served at the bar and how they had to call the police on them.

He asks how I am holding up; I ask if he's being careful. Near the end of the meal, Dean receives a call from work about a fire. He asks if I will be okay walking home alone because he needs to run back to his car and get to the station as fast as he can.

After I reassure him I will be fine, he drops enough to cover the bill, tip and then some on the table and with a quick kiss I tell him to go. I watch out the window as he trots off back toward my apartment, hoping he stays safe. Soon after he rushes off, the waiter returns and I pay the bill. On my walk home, I decide to take a trip out to Manhattan where the shop on the card is, so I can purchase a couple of items I tried out the previous night at the club. Originally I was going to spend more time with Dean, inviting him back to the apartment for a little quality time, but his call cancelled that. Now that I have some free time, I might as well make the best of it and I still have the keys to Betty's car.

When I get to the store, I am a little nervous going in. There are gates across all the windows, and the glass is painted black with the name of the store in big red letters outlined in white. Stepping in, I am relieved to see how well lit it is, and I wander around looking at everything they have to offer. My main purchase is going to be the electric body clamps kit with detachable and interchangeable length wires. It was not quite like the one the man that attacked me had, but I believes his may have been homemade or at least modified. As I wander through the store some more, I come across a section with acupuncture supplies and it peaks my attention. I had watched a cheesy horror movie once where the killer used an acupuncture needle to paralyze their victims. Wondering if it is possible, I start to finger through a couple of the books. After reading that it is indeed possible, I decide on a book called *Acupuncture: A Comprehensive Text* as well as a couple packages of needles and a quick guide booklet of all the main points on the body. I set my items down on the counter and head back to grab a pair of fur lined leather cuffs, a black satin blindfold and decide to get a flail to complete the appearance my purchase is for extracurricular activities. The clerk rings everything up and I pay with cash. He then puts my items into a couple of plain paper bags like the ones you get at the grocery store, folding the tops down slightly and then hands the bags to me.

With a smile and a "Good day" I head out, ignoring the grin the clerk was wearing on his face as he checked me out. I am dressed like an innocent maiden, so who knows what sort of thoughts are going through his head.

As I reach the car, a thought crosses my mind, how will I transport these things to and from the site without being noticed? I cannot just walk around with paper bags every time I need to go do a job. Placing the bag in the trunk I head over to a boutique just down the block and look over the wide selection of bags and purses. I need something large, preferably with lots of pockets to sort and hide things in. Finally I find the perfect one; it is a large black leather purse with handles as well as a removable shoulder strap. Inside, there are multiple pockets and the main section is split into two sides. Without even looking at the price tag I take it up to the register and pay for it, again with cash. When I return to the car, I carefully transfer most of the items from the paper bag to the new purse, leaving the books in one of the bags. I decide to leave the purse in the trunk and get in the driver's seat to head home. On my way back, I stop and fill the gas tank up as I always do before returning it. On my way in I return the keys to Betty who gives me a big smile and asks if I took care of all my errands. Smiling back and letting her know that I did and thanking her again, I head up to my apartment with the purse draped over one arm and the paper bag tucked under the other.

Back in the apartment, I lock all the locks, including the chain on my front door and head into my bedroom to check out my new tools. Carefully, I remove each one and look it over, arranging them on my bed. I go into the bathroom and pull out the Ziploc bag of make-up, placing them in one of the outside pockets where they would be easily reachable. I then zip it up and return to the bed. Looking at the electric device with its accessories, as well as the needles and guide, I wonder if I need more tools for my kit. A folding knife of some sort would be good, just in case, some plastic zip ties and a roll of duct tape, as well. Heading out to my living room, I pull out my fishing tackle box of tools and take out a hunting knife my father gave my when I first moved into an apartment alone, as well as a partially used roll of duct tape and a handful of long zip ties. As I place the box back in the closet, I grab a handful of medical gloves from my art supplies box. I leave the stuff on the floor and head into the kitchen to grab a large baggie and go back in, placing the gloves and ties into it. I look at the tape and decide to try and flatten the roll so it will fit better in my purse. Since it was over half gone, I was able to flatten it enough and tucked it into the bag. Heading back to my room, I tuck the bag in the pocket with my makeup. One of the outer pockets has slots for credit cards, so I clip the knife onto the uppermost pocket so that I can easily find it in an emergency.

Setting the purse aside temporarily, I decide to test the shock toy to ensure it works properly. I would hate to have everything set up, have the criminal, and find out it is defective. I sit at the edge of my bed and set the box beside me. Clipping one of the alligator clips on my pinky and flipping the device on, I run through the settings and it works exactly like the one at the club. Satisfied, I place it and its accessories in the other large pocket, as well as a small package of replacement batteries. The purse is starting to look a little full but I am not done yet. I look at the needles and decide to leave them and the books out for now, at least until I have had a chance to explore them somewhat. Lying back against a pile of pillow on my bed, I read through the book, studying the chapter on finding points and proper application and scanning through the rest. I use the quick guide to make notes, with a red pen marking the important points for what I will be doing. After I finish the book,, I decide to test it out a little. Pulling out a small sealed package from the box of needles I carefully peel open the packet to expose the blunt end. The needle is so thin I wonder how it could possibly do anything but when I place it in the point that controls pain in the feet, I realize the effectiveness of it. After placing two more needles in their appropriate points, I sit back and enjoyed the relief I feel. My feet had been so sore from those boots, I had a difficult time walking today, but now they are pain free. When I remove the needles, I noticed there are no marks at all to show they were even there. This excites me, because it means I would not have to hide my use of them. After disposing of the needles, I pack the box into an empty Altoids tin to disguise them. I put the pins and the guide in the purse and then tuck it into the hiding place in the bathroom on top of the lockbox.

Looking at the clock, I realize it's almost time for Dean to get off his shift, so I decide to meet him at the station house for a surprise late dinner at the nearby pizza place. Securing everything away, I head to the stop on the corner and give him a call while waiting for my bus.

Dean offers to give me a ride but I point out that if I take the bus, I will get there no later than five minutes after his shift is up, if he comes to get me than we have to wait that much longer to eat.

With a laugh, he agrees and with a "See you in 20", hangs up just as the bus pulls up. I tuck my phone in my pocket and board, dropping the exact change into the little box.

I find a seat next to a little elderly lady who briefly looks away from the window to give me a nod and then goes back to staring outside. I sit down and accompany the woman in watching out the window, thinking about what I learned, as well as about how worn out Dean sounded on the phone. As we arrive on the block of the firehouse, I can see Dean waiting for me at the sign and reach up to ding the bell letting the driver know I want to get off. As I step off the bus, Dean lifts me off the ground in a big hug and gives me a kiss, bringing a howl from the group of young passengers at the front of the bus. Blushing, I slap him in the arm and grab his hand, leading him away from the bus and toward the pizzeria while scolding him playfully.

When we sit down at a table near the front window and order our meals, I notice Dean seems more worn out than usual and although he is trying to hide it, something is on his mind. I slide out of my seat and onto the booth seat next to him and grab his hand.

He gives me a tired smile, and I reach my other hand up to touch his face and ask what is wrong.

At first he doesn't respond, so I give his hand a squeeze of encouragement and he proceeds to tell me about the fire they had to deal with today.

It was in one of the older complexes in the low-income district and there was a family with three children trapped in a fifth floor apartment. The fire had consumed the bottom two floors and they were unable to get to the apartment from below so they tried to use the ladder but the gates on the windows were old and rusted and were refusing to open. By the time they cut through the gate, the youngest had passed out from smoke inhalation but luckily they got them all out. The parents were nowhere to be found and all the children were all under the age of ten. Dean could not understand how a parent could just leave their children alone like that.

Tears threatened to escape my eyes and I looked into his face. He wants to believe in the good in everyone, but times like this prove it is not possible. I give him a big hug and he pulls my tight against him, holding me so tight it was almost difficult to breathe. When I let out a squeak of discomfort, he loosens up a little but continues to hold me until the food arrives. When the waiter sets the meal on the table he reluctantly lets go but puts his hand on my leg when I go to move back to the other side. Seeing he needs me near, I stay there and we start to eat in silence.

After he finishes off his first slice, something seems to change in him. He sits up straight and tells me that after dinner he is just going to go back to his place and that he hopes I am not disappointed.

When I let him know I completely understand, he continues to ask if I mind skipping their morning workout as well. Concerned, I put my hand over his, giving it a squeeze and tell him to take all the time he needs and that I am there if he needs me. I am not one to give advice about how to cope, so I just offer to be supportive and let him deal in his own way. After filling up on pizza, Dean gives me a ride home and walks me to the door of the building, leaving the car out front in view.

He apologizes again for not being able to stay the night, but explains that he needs to go home and work off the anger he is feeling.

I give him a soft kiss on the lips, stroking his cheek comfortingly and let him know I understand. He gives another tight hug and trails his hands down my arms and squeezes my hands before turning to get back to the car. From the driver's seat, he leans down to wave to me and I wave back as he drives off.

After watching him turn the corner, I head up to my apartment and ponder whether I want to rehabilitate the rapist tonight or perform a little reconnaissance work. I am eager to serve him justice but this is my first time and I want to be sure I get it right. After a little more thought, I decide to do recon tonight after all. I cannot let my pain from Dean's story make me move too fast and do something reckless. I change into a pair of black jeans and a black tee shirt and grab my black cabbie hat and head for the bathroom. There, I tuck my hair up into the cap as best I can, using a few bobby pins to hold it in place and head back to my bedroom to put on my boots. I tie a black silk scarf around my waist so that I can tie it around my neck and face when I get there to hide my identity and blend into the shadows better. Looking in the mirror, I question if the outfit would pass as 'work attire' and decide it will. Grabbing the keys and tucking my wallet in my back pocket I head out, locking up on my way out.

As I reach the lobby, I run into a young man that lives a couple floors down from me. We occasionally meet on the elevator and he seems to think that it gives him the right to make a comment on my new look and informs me it will definitely be earning more tips.

With a snarky "Thanks", I continue out the door and head to the house the rapist uses as a hide-out.

Sticking to the shadows, I make my way behind the house and transfer the scarf to my face and head. At first, I walk the perimeter, rechecking the openings as well as danger zones. The lights are all off inside, so I knows he is not here yet. I look at my watch and wonder if I have time to check inside, when I see a light come on in a room a couple windows away from me. Quickly but carefully, I make my way to the window and peek in to see him hiding the knife again. The lantern is on the floor near him. He moves through a doorway to the left and I move to the window nearest it, careful to stay out of the glow from the light. He is now in the kitchen and I watch him open the old refrigerator door and pull out a bottle of vodka and a box. He then moves back into the first room and sits on an old mattress he has propped in the corner like a makeshift couch. He sets the box beside him. Opening it he pulls out a pipe and a baggy with little crystals in it. I watch as he packs the crystals into the pipe and using a blue flamed lighter smokes whatever it is, followed by a gulp of the vodka. I make note of this and keep it in consideration as well as the smoking the last time. I am assured he is the only one that uses this place, since he would not leave his booze and drugs in it as he does if there was anyone else coming and going. This is a good sign, it means I can come a little early and prepare the scene. I watch him waste nearly an hour, sitting there with his drugs and drink before he gets up and puts them back in the refrigerator. He then goes back into the room with the mattress and pulls a girly magazine out from under the mattress and opens his pants. I look away because I am really not interested in what he plans to do. When I hear him make a grunting sound followed by silence, I take a quick glance and see him wiping his hands on the mattress. Fighting the urge to vomit, I turn away and that is when an idea springs to my head. I make a note in my book and look back up in time to see him heading back into the kitchen. He heads to the fridge and opens it up. He turns the light out and I hear the thunk of the fridge closing, followed by the back door. Quickly, I peek around and watch him stash a key under a bush to the left of the doorway and now I know how to get in easily and without detection, as well as keep the place secure. I follow him back to his apartment and then return to the house, where I let myself in and check out the layout once again but this time a little more in depth. Carefully, I look in the cabinets and other areas where things could be hidden, ensuring there will be no surprises when I return the following night. After making notes of all the important things, I tuck my book back into my pocket and head out, locking up and putting the key back where I found it. Before heading out, I remove my scarf from my head and retie it around my waist. As soon as I get home, I stash the notebook, shower and head to bed where sleep quickly takes hold.

Chapter 9

Although I went to bed around two this morning, I still woke at six. My mind is reeling and ready to go, even though my body is still tired. Since I am up, I decided to go to the gym and get in a workout. It would not be good to miss two days in a row now that I have a plan in place. After my normal routine at the gym, I head back to my apartment and shower. The entire time I was working out, I thought about what I planned to do tonight. My mind played through numerous scenarios and finally I decide to use his drugs, alcohol and sexual desires toward his undoing. I also plan to make him feel everything he made each of those women feel, all at once. Fear, pain, helplessness. When I am finished with him, he will not only regret what he did, he will never be able to look at another woman in the same way again. I will make him pay in such a way he will not only be punished for his crimes, but he will be cured of the desire to do them again. With that thought in mind, I decide to go to the YMCA after getting cleaned up, so that I can fuel the fires inside me pushing me toward this task.

I walk in the building and head downstairs to the room marked 'Support Group Meeting Room'. Entering it, I see several of the old faces and a couple new ones. Making my rounds, I say hello to all my friends and introduce myself to the new faces. I noticed that one of the new faces looked familiar, and then I realized it was the woman I saved. She glanced at me but did not recognize me. I sighed in relief and then approached her.

Her name is Jennie and she recently moved here from a small town upstate; she is going to college here for music. Her eyes fill with tears as she admits she intends to drop out and go home.

I take her hand and give it a squeeze and tell her she is safe now, but she does not believe me.

She tells me he is still out there, and as long as he is, no woman is safe. I tell her about my experience and how I learned to cope with the fear and she just stares at me in awe. She asks if I am afraid, and

I admit that "Yes I am a little, but that I will not let that fear rule my life." When the meeting starts she sits next to me, and the woman hosting today introduces her to the others. As normal, we go around the room and share our stories. Women with similar tales begin to congregate together and afterwards, they all sit around and console each other. I excuse myself and go to the ladies room and quickly write down all the names of the women that were attacked by that rapist, and then I return in time for the cookies and coffee. When everyone starts leaving I make my final rounds and head home myself.

When I return home from the meeting, I have lost all doubts about what I plan to do. The man was total scum and deserves to be punished! My mind set, I pull out my supplies and go through them once more, making sure I have everything I will need for this evening. As I look over the clips for the shock machine, I decide they might not work for what I wish to use it for so I ponder alternatives. I know where I intend to use the clip, which is a highly sensitive area of the body and not any place that I could easily clip something. I rack my mind for ideas. At first I consider wrapping it in copper wire, but it would be time consuming on the spot and possibly leave marks. If I make something ahead of time, it may not fit properly. Suddenly I remember seeing sheets of thin metal foil at the hardware store, and a light bulb goes on in my head. I remember the stuff is made for spreading an electrical current evenly over a larger area. Excited, I get up, tucking everything back away and head to the hardware store where I pick up a couple sheets of metal as well as a packet of rubber sheets about the size of a postcard. Heading home, I attach one of the metal sheets to the rubber ones in order to insulate the metal and protect areas outside my target zone from it. Carefully I pack the new supplies into the bag, along with a handful of rubber bands and tuck them away. I pull the book on acupuncture off the shelf between my living-room windows and sit down with it to refresh myself on technique, as well as safety. I scan the different chapters and makes notes of different points that would come in handy at a later date.

As I place the book back on the shelf, I decide to have an early dinner with Dean, using the excuse of being called in to cover a shift at the bar. Although my mind is not on happy fuzzy thoughts at the moment, I know that if I do not at least attempt to live a "normal" life, someone may become suspicious. Besides, Dean is the only tether keeping me grounded, keeping me from going over the edge. He answers on the second ring and tells me he is glad I called, since he feels bad about yesterday. I explain why I was calling and he tells me he will be happy with whatever time he can have with me. He says he cannot wait to see me and invites me to dinner at his place, and then we hang up.

I get myself dressed up and head over to his apartment, where I am greeted by mouthwatering scents. I am amazed by the fact he cooked the meal himself and managed to get it done in the forty-five minutes it took me to get ready and get there, and it is spectacular. He prepared chicken parmesan over linguini with a small salad and cheese-covered garlic French bread on the side. I knew I should not eat too much with my plans for the evening, but the food was so tasty, I just had to finish off my serving. After dinner, I thanked him, gave him a big hug and then apologized for having to leave, before heading home.

When I return home I begin to prepare myself both mentally and physically for the evening. First, I sit down and look at all the pictures of the poor women he attacked. I read the articles, taking to memory the stories within, as well as the ones told to me just earlier today. My fury rises and the last thing I do is head for the shower. I scrub my entire body down with a slightly rough natural loofa sponge meant for clearing off dead skin. This is to limit the amount of dry flakes that may fall off my body on the scene. After drying off, I use a moisturizer on my entire body and prepare my hair while it absorbs into my skin. Finally, I dress in a black long sleeve tee and black jeans. I finish off the ensemble with my boots.

Grabbing my purse, I head for the door with a small backpack over one shoulder and my supply purse in the other. My hair is tucked up in the wig cap, and I place a fairly large floppy hat over it to hide the fabric of the cap. I want to be sure not to leave any hair behind, so I tuck it all away, wrapping it in plastic wrap after pinning it up but before placing the cap on. I then head out and go to the place where the rapist hides out. I make sure to get there ahead of time, pretty sure he will be showing up some time between eleven and twelve that evening. The first thing I do is retrieve his knife and check to be sure his things are still in the refrigerator. Then, I head into the room he seems to spend the most time in. On the wall next to the mattress, I tape the pictures of the women he attacked. Beneath them, I jab his knife into the mattress next to a disgusting stain I can only assume is what he left behind during my last stake-out. With his habit of wiping his hands on the mattress afterwards, I am sure his DNA is all over the place already, so I would not have to find a way to add more. With the pictures on the wall, it makes it appear he was using images of his victims to get off to and pulling out the magazine, I even tape some ripped out images of their faces over the ones of the women in the magazine and tuck it back under the mattress. Originally, I planned to put his drugs and booze in there as well, but then I decided he might be tipped off if they are not in the refrigerator with his lantern, so I changed my mind. I can move them after he is secured in his place on the mattress. Looking at the room, I am satisfied, so I go stash my supplies for the rehabilitation session in a cabinet in the kitchen behind some trash.

After I finish setting up I make sure I have not left any sign of my presence besides the obvious ones and then head to the bathroom to prepare. I transform into my new persona like a caterpillar morphs into a butterfly, taking extra care with the make-up and wig. I want to be sure there is no way he would recognize me in the future. Looking over myself in the grubby broken mirror, I do not recognize the person looking back. She is darker, angrier and ready to teach someone a lesson. Once I am done, I hide in a closet close to the entry point I watched him use the previous times I saw him enter the building. I realize I have cut it close when he enters and heads straight for the fridge to get his light, moments after I closed the door and clicked off my own light. He follows his routine to a tee and when he comes back into the kitchen to put his drugs away, I quietly follow him back into the other room. He is completely oblivious to the images on the wall and I wonder if he was already toasted before he even arrived. As the previous time, he lies down on the mattress and grabs his magazine and looks at the images before exposing himself and closing his eyes. As soon as he closes them, I spring into action and stick him with the paralyzing pin. He jerks and his eyes fly open but before he can make a sound, I place the second needle. He is unable to move, and now he is unable to make a sound. Grinning at my success, I look down at him, placing the final needle in his skin in a secondary point for paralysis. Once I am satisfied he cannot move, I head to the kitchen to get my tools.

When I return to the room, I rotate his head so he is facing the pictures on the wall.

"Do you know what you did to them?" I ask as I grab his throat and give a little squeeze.

His eyes twitch but he is unable to respond. Still holding him, I whisper in his ear "You made them feel helpless, afraid... Kinda like I am sure you feel right now."

Releasing his throat, I settle back and open my bag just within the very edge of his vision. Slowly, I open the zipper, letting him wonder what is coming. His head is facing slightly away from me but I can see his eyes cranked as far as they will go in my direction. I let out a soft giggle as I pull out the shock device with one hand and turn his head toward me with the other.

"Do you see this? Bet you have no idea what it is, do you? It's a neat little machine that delivers an electric shock through these" holding up one of the clips I open and close it.

"That can be clipped anywhere on your body. However, I don't want to leave any marks, so I came up with an idea."

With that, I pull out the bag with my metal and rubber sheet. I explain to the man that it is a super thin sheet metal, flexible as foil but stronger and so much more conductive, attached to a sheet of rubber for insulation. I carefully slide them under his now-flaccid member with the metal side up and wrap them around him and secure them with a couple rubber bands. Although I am careful not to make contact with his skin with my hands, he still reacts to my touch and expands within the tightened device. The rubber bands allow for expansion while keeping it snug.

Glad he is completely covered by my makeshift sleeve, I move closer to his ear again and inform him "You've used that thing to traumatize so many women. You impaled them with it against their will, while taking away their ability to defend themselves. You caused them deep emotional pain and still they suffer from it! Now you will know the same kind of pain. You will know suffering, shame and horror at the hands of another."

As I speak the end of that last sentence, I turn the machine on and a trickle of electrical current flows down the wires into the metal sheath. I watch as his eyes twitch slightly but it is not the reaction I was hoping for, so slowly I increase the voltage to half way. This is when tears start to flow down his face and I can see that he is no longer enjoying the attention. Now, this is more of what I was hoping for.

As he sits there feeling the pain and unable to move, I tell him "You will **never** touch another woman like that again, or I will find you and next time I will not be so gentle."

Seeing the tears flowing harder now, I check the edges of the sheath to ensure it is not causing any physical damage like burning his skin or pinching, before I snap the dial up to high for only a couple seconds before turning it off. The man would have screamed if he was able but instead his eyes roll up into his head and he passes out.

Standing over him, I look at him lying there passed out from the shock and I feel the anger and hatred flow away from me. I suddenly feel better and I even smile as I remove the sheath and place his left hand over the exposed skin, covering the offending weapon. I turn his head toward the images; place the open magazine on his lap. Placing the sheath in a bag to be disposed of, and the rest of my tools back in the bag, I head to the kitchen. There, I find a bottle of really cheap vodka in the refrigerator, so I return with it and his box of drugs. Dribbling some of the vodka over the front of his clothing, as well as pouring some into his mouth and forcing him to swallow it down, I then place the bottle in his hand and let them fall back so that the mouth of the bottle lands beyond the edge of the mattress. This way, the Vodka does not chance washing away the evidence he has left on the mattress. Instead, it pours across the floor, soaking into the underside of the mattress and dripping through the floorboards. I ensure he is still passed out before carefully removing the needles and placing them in a small baggie in the Altoids tin. I tuck the last of my things back into the bag, slinging it over my shoulder and look down at him. I step back and look at the entire scene and realize he probably does not have enough of either the drugs or alcohol in his system to validate the story I have presented. I look down at the box and open it up. There are several types of drugs in there, but the only one I have any idea of how it's ingested requires inhalation. That is when I see the needle with a small amount of something in it. I hope I will succeed as I tie the rubber cord around his arm and wait for the veins to pop out, and then I insert the needle near a cluster of puncture marks and depress the plunger. Removing the needle, I drop it on the mattress beside him and check his pulse to be sure he is still alive and that I did not accidentally kill him with an overdose.

When I am finished setting the scene, I open the front door slightly and begin screaming. When I hear footsteps, I loudly run out the back, pretending to be a scared witness or perhaps lover that stumbled across the scene but that does not want to be caught. From a safe distance slightly down the block and across the street, I watch the people looking in and see one of them pulls out his cell. It is not long before the police arrive and find him still lying there among the images of his victims in a very compromising position.

Shortly after the police arrive they help him regain consciousness and starts screaming about "A crazy bitch" and how he "Aint admitting to nut'in!"

Finally, I watch as they take him away in cuffs, his expression is one of confusion, fear and anger as he scans the onlookers for the woman that did this to him. He cannot see me, but I can see him, and I can see the fear in his eyes. No, he will not be hurting another woman again.

After a very productive evening, I decide to go home and get myself cleaned up and changed into my normal attire. I am full of energy and life after my successful first attempt and decide I need to celebrate, so I head down to the tavern where I work and have a couple drinks. I tell my boss that I was out taking a walk since I could not sleep, when a whole lot of crazy happened just a few blocks away. I share what I heard and saw and that I could not believe they finally caught that piece of dirt again and that I sure hope they do not let him out again anytime soon. It is a little before closing time when my cell phone rings, looking down I see that it is Dean. When I answer, I allow him to hear some of the background noise in the bar before stepping outside to hear him better.

I ask if everything is okay and he asks me the same thing. I question what he means and he tells me that the story all over the news and how the guy was not far from where I was working.

I let him know that I am fine and ask if he wants to pick me up and give me a ride home.

I can hear the relief in his voice when he tells me he will be here by the time I'm done closing up, and I hope he gets there after the boss-man leaves.

I head back inside and offer to help clean up a little and I get the "It's your night off" speech, as he hands me the mop.

With a laugh, I start cleaning up in front of the bar while he wipes down the tables and stacks the chairs on top of them. While he's finishing up behind the bar, I clean up the rest of the floor and check the bathrooms.

We get the place cleaned up in record time, and he asks if my ride is here yet.

I look out but do not see Dean's car, so I shake my head.

Worried about my safety, he tells me I can wait inside the door but to be sure to lock up and pull the gate before I leave.

Thanking him, I lock the door behind him and watch down the street for my ride. Dean pulls up to the curb and gives me a big grin before getting out and striding up to give me a big hug from behind, as I am locking the door. After I pull the gate down and click the lock in place, he grabs me and pulls me into a strong embrace. Before I have a chance to question it, he gives me a big kiss and tells me he is so glad to see me safe.

We ride home, talking about the take-down and Dean tells me how he is so glad they finally got another one of those miscreants off the street. I pick on him about the 'big word' he used and he just sticks his tongue out at me and continues driving.

We get back to my apartment, and I notice there is a smear of black on the bathroom door knob.

Before I have a chance to determine what it is, Dean points it out and asks if I started another painting.

A moment of panic hits before I come up with a reason that both covers the smear and explains why there is no painting. I let out a long exasperated sigh and tell him I tried but that it got me so frustrated, I threw it down the incinerator. It would not have been the first time I did this, so it did not surprise him, he just shook his head as I used a clump of damp toilet paper to wipe the handle down. As I flush them down the toilet, I hope that I did not miss anything else in my haste. I ask him to put on a pot of water for me, since I could use a cup of tea and tell him I want to change into something a bit more comfortable.

He laughs and asks if I mean *comfortable* or comfortable and I give him a smack on the arm and shove him toward the kitchen.

When I see him enter the kitchen, I quickly look around the bathroom, making sure my area was closed up and nothing was sitting around. After a brief inspection, I head to my room, closing the door behind me. I see my make-up bag sitting on the dresser and I quickly grab it and shove it into my drawer with my pajamas, pulling out my favorite pair at the same time. Slowly, I rotate; examining the room to be sure nothing else was left out and seeing it is clear, let out the breath I did not even realize I was holding. After changing, I head into the kitchen to find Dean had pulled out two mugs and placed them on the counter, one had a tea bag already in it, the other was empty.

As soon as I enter he puts on a false sad face and says "oh… comfortable" in a dejected tone.

I ask if he wants another whack and he laughs and then asks what type of tea I want.

Just as he reaches into the cabinet for my Sweet Dreams, the pot begins to whistle. I slide past him, allowing myself to glide across his back and reach for the knob, turning off the flame. I then slide back behind him, wrapping my arms around him giving him a big hug, pressing my face between his shoulder blades and drinking in his scent before moving back to the table. Dean pours the water into our mugs and brings them to the table before retrieving the honey and a spoon. After finishing our tea, Dean and I take turns brushing our teeth and head to my bedroom. Climbing into bed I cuddle into the strength of his arms, and for a brief moment, all is right in the world. Without another thought I fall asleep in his arms.

Chapter 10

I found that after doing what I had done, I did not feel guilt or regret. Instead, it was almost therapeutic and I now felt less afraid. I reviewed how everything went and decided there were a few minor glitches last night. I will need to plan things better for next time, and maybe not rush into it like I did; both for the process and cover-up. Waking up next to Dean I remember my mistakes and how close I came to being caught, or at least put under suspicion, and realized I need to plan for a visit from him at all times, either that or I had to walk away from him for good. Laying there in his strong arms, his breath against the back of my neck, I knew I could not walk away, so I had to be more careful. After thinking some more, I figure out I need to make up some lists and lay out a plan.

Not long afterwards, Dean starts to stir and giving me a big squeeze, asks what time it is.

When I tell him, he quickly sits up and says he needs to get home and ready for work.

I pout and ask if he has time for breakfast, but he tells me he needs to be on the clock in two hours.

Sadly, I tell him I understand and watch as he pulls on his jeans and shirt that he draped over a chair the night before.

He then sits at the foot of the bed and pulls on his socks before giving me a kiss and whispers "See you later" in my ear before he runs out the door.

I can hear the latching of my locks and sigh before getting out of bed myself. I head in to the bathroom first and take a shower then grab a quick breakfast. Not wanting to possibly be caught planning at home I then head to a park with my notebook and a smile. Last night, I took down a rapist the police have been tracking for months, and I am fairly certain I rehabilitated him better than any jail could ever dream. Then, I came home with a handsome, caring man and we had an amazing night together. Life could not get any better... Well, other than getting my revenge on the evil man.

Walking through the park, I find a nice secluded place where my back is against a tall wooden barrier along the highway and I am facing out so I can keep a solid awareness of my environment yet work in peace. I pull a small blanket from my bag and spread it out on the ground and sitting down on it, pull my bag into my lap. I take a moment to look around at the absolute beauty of the park. The trees are full of leaves, the air is crisp and clean, everything so serene and restful. I close my eyes and take a slow long breath and then when I open them, I am focused and ready to get to work. Pulling out the article printouts from the newspaper about my abduction, I set them to my left, and then my notes and drawings from the warehouse, on my right. There is a chance I may practice on another abuser before my final task; I want to be sure I am fully prepared for when the opportunity arises to complete my plans. With notes in hand, I start on my lists so that everything will be perfect. I split a sheet of paper into two halves and write at the top of each half, what each list is. I then go through my notes and add to the list what I will need. At first, I start building my list based off what he did to me, but then I decided to use my new knowledge and be creative in my torture of him. After several hours and lots of adding, crossing out, reading, and changing, I finally have my complete list.

Type of Environment:
- Large open area, inside far from people
- Tall ceilings
- Objects to utilize
- Chain and hook
- Natural light & candles
- Easy to clean afterwards
Tools:
- Long rubber gloves, black hooded robes, Chinese-style slippers and metal finger claws
- Ropes, duct tape and gag
- Incense
- MP3 Player with speakers
- Towel
- Case or bag with:
  - Acupuncture needles and scroll with point placements in a pouch
  - Electro-shock device, alligator clips, fish hooks and spool of

conductive wire
- Piercing gun, hoops and dagger charms
- Exacto knife, scouring pad and bottle of lemon juice
- Stone bowl and torch oil
- Can of flammable liquid and matches
- Bleach and rags

I make a note to look into super charging the machine somehow, it needs more juice if it is going to compare to the one he used on me, and play with some ideas and scenarios. I write each one on a different sheet of paper so I can pick and choose what I want to do. When I am done, I tuck everything carefully into my messenger bag and then sit there enjoying the peacefulness of the park for a bit. Holding my bag under my arm, I lean back against the fence, closing my eyes and turning my face upward to feel the sun warm it. For a moment, I wonder if I am doing the right thing. What would Dean think of me if he found my notes? How am I going to feel about myself after I am done? So many questions running through my thoughts and for the briefest moment, doubt appears. As the sun begins to heat my cheeks, a flashback hits me; I am lying on the ground, bloody and hurting. I am battered and abused and filled with fear, wishing for death all alone. At that moment, when the fear and panic swell, all doubt disappears. What needs to be done is he needs to be stopped and I will do it, no matter what the cost. I think about how much he hurt me and how much I wish to return the 'favor'. Right now, the only things I have are Dean, and my need for revenge, and unfortunately my need to release my revenge outweighs my love for Dean which I am keeping at bay until my soul is freed from its dark prison. I sit in my peaceful hideaway, lost in thought for quite a while. The sun is starting to set and I pull out my cell phone to check the time.

Realizing I have just a little over an hour before my date with Dean, I jump up and rush home. The bus seems to take longer than usual, leaving me very little time once I actually reach the apartment. When I get there, I quickly tuck the book and papers into the lock box, hiding it away and then take a brief shower and get dressed. Dean arrives on time, as usual, and I give him a hug and a kiss at the door and invite him in. It has been a while since our last true date, so Dean decided we were due for one. Originally we were going to do what has become our traditional dinner and a movie in, but I decide I want to kick it up a little and actually 'go out' this time. I take him by the hand and lead him over to the couch where we cuddle together and look at the weekly movie guide from the Sunday paper.

After a short debate, we choose a new movie with a bunch of starting actors. Neither of us has heard of the movie, but the description sounds promising, and with it not being a blockbuster movie, it means the theater will hopefully not be too crowded.

For dinner, we decide on a little Italian restaurant just down the street from the movie theater, since Italian is my favorite and Dean tells me he has no preference.

We pick up our tickets before heading to dinner to avoid possible lines after the meal and then head to the restaurant. Deciding to walk the couple blocks since it is such a lovely evening, Dean takes my arm and I lean into him.

As we walk, he tells me about how, when he was a kid, he used to imagine walking down the street with his parents, holding hands and happy. I stop him and give him a soft, affectionate kiss, running my hand across his slightly rough cheek.

His beard seems to grow so fast, and by this time of day, the stubble is quite visible. We stand there a few moments, gazing at each other before the moment is ruined by a loud grumble from my stomach. With a laugh,

Dean takes my hand and says "Let's feed that monster before it escapes" and whisks me off to the restaurant.

When we arrive at the restaurant, the waiter brings us to our table and we sit down across from each other. He hands us our menus, spouting out the specials and the wines of the day. Before "giving us time to decide" he asks if we would like anything to drink, so I decide to order a glass of wine with my dinner.

Since we are walking to the theater and the movie was nearly two hours long, Dean decides to join me in the wine.

I order a sweet white and Dean gets a dry red. As the waiter heads off to get our wines, we look at the menu and my face goes ashen. When I picked the restaurant I did not realize it was so expensive.

As if picking up on my thoughts, Dean reaches across the table and touches my hand which is gripping the edge of the table. I look up at him and he tells me not to worry about it, he will take care of it.

Still overwhelmed by the cost, I decide on the spaghetti with handmade meatballs and red sauce, and they better be amazing meatballs for nearly twenty three dollars. Dean orders the angel hair pasta with grilled Italian sausage and a garlic red sauce, as well as a side of bread sticks and salad for us both.

We sit and hold idle conversations about work, life and other general things while we wait for the meals to arrive. As we sit here talking about the same old things, I wonder where things are going between us. I want to move forward but cannot until I finish my task, but I do not know how long I can keep Dean at arm's length, especially after last night.

As if picking up on my thoughts he reaches across the table and takes my hand. I look down at his hand and then up at his face. He looks concerned and I cannot understand why until he repeats the question he had asked.

I had been so lost in my thoughts that I did not hear him ask if I wanted to join him for a weekend trip upstate. He has to go for a training session, but there would be time for social activities. Smiling,

I tell him I will need to ask my boss since I am scheduled to work this weekend but that I will try and get the time off. He gives my hand a squeeze before I take it back and pull out my cell. Hitting the speed dial for the bar, I have a quick conversation that ends in disappointment.

'The man' as I refer to him, told me it's too late to get the time off since I am the only one that was even available to work that shift.

Sighing, I give Dean the bad news even though he could read it all over my face and although disappointed, he tells me it is okay. He tells me he could hear my boss yelling and apologies for possibly getting me into trouble.

I see the disappointment on his face, even though he tries to hide it, and it twists something in my heart. We eat the rest of our meal in silence but with occasional glances and touches. When we are done, Dean pays the bill and as we walk out of the restaurant, he slides his arm around my waist and we head to the movie. When we walk into the theater, it's nearly empty, and remains that way. We get perfect seats center isle and just far enough from the screen that we can take it all in without being too far away. Leaning in my seat as far as the armrest allows, I try to cuddle up to Dean while he has his arm wrapped around my shoulders. I cannot understand the twinge that is pulling at my heart, but I feel as if somehow I have done something wrong. After the movie, I invite him back to my place. At the door, I take his hand and pull him inside, locking the door up behind him. Surprise clear on his face as I move in for a passionate kiss. Before he has a chance to go all chivalrous, I turn him and push him into my bedroom, working the buttons on his shirt and using my foot to slam the door closed behind us.

The next morning, I wake up to find myself in Dean's strong arms. He has been up for a bit but did not want to disturb me. As my eyes focus on his face, I feel his hand caress my cheek and gently slide down my neck. Closing my eyes I enjoy the feeling and when I open them, I can see his eyes filled with so many questions. I know he will not ask them however because I will just clam up and push him away again, so he just savors the moment. After a short time, he glances at the clock regretfully tells me he will need to get going in about an hour so that he has time to go home and change before starting his shift. His hand that was on my lower back slides down a little as he pulls me against him and kisses my neck before he gets up. Slowly, I get out of bed and head to the bathroom to quickly wash up and brush my teeth. I then head into the kitchen with just my robe on and start cooking up some scrambled eggs and sausages while Dean cleans up. As Dean walks into the kitchen, the toaster pops up and he takes the toast and places it on our plates. Bringing the plates to me, I serve each of us some eggs and sausage and we sit at the table together. Distracted from his food, Dean cannot believe I am sitting across from him in my robe after spending the night together. He dreamed of this for so long and now that it is finally happening, he wonders if it is all a dream. Seeing the strange expression he is wearing, I fling a piece of egg at him.

"Would you eat before it gets cold" I exclaim and he bursts into laughter quickly shoving a forkful into his mouth.

As I sit there with a smile on my face, I wonder if this is what it is like to live a normal life. Maybe someday I can find out. After breakfast, Dean helps with clean-up, washing the pans and loading the dishwasher. As he gets ready to leave, he pulls me close and kisses me passionately and then heads out the door. He bends down and picks up the paper, setting it on my little table before blowing me a kiss and shutting the door. I lock the door behind him and head in to take my shower.

After a long hot shower, I dress and grabbing the paper, head into the living-room to sit and read. Opening the paper, I am thrown into shock by the headline. GOWANUS BAY BUTCHER ATTACKS AGAIN! There it is, in front of my eyes, my worst fear. My heart stops as panic threaten to take over. My breaths come in short bursts until the anger kicks in. The rage bubbles up from deep within me as I continue to read the article, swallowing the fear and feeding it to the darkness swirling below the surface. Determined to find him now, I start planning my revenge in full force. I need to find this man and proceed with my plans before he hurts another woman. I **will** take him down. I must! Having taken on hiking as my 'new favorite activity' I have the perfect excuse to take day trips to different places, and even a weekend excursion or two if necessary. With Dean's schedule, he would not be able to go with me, making it the perfect cover. First thing I will need to do is secure a location so that when I finally find him, I know where I will be taking him. Pulling out my laptop, I do some searches, combining hiking trails and scenic areas into my search so as to hide any foul motives. I come across several old buildings that would be ideal, ranging from abandoned schoolhouses to churches, but will need to narrow down the list some. I decided to take this weekend to look each of them over and make a decision. My plan is to watch each of the properties for a couple consecutive nights to see if anyone uses the building for any reason. Since Dean will be gone this entire weekend starting Thursday night, it will be the perfect time. I know I have to work, but I can check the place out before and after work with no problems. Right now, however, I need to do something else. Opening up a new search page, I look for places close-by to get a tattoo. Finding several, I start making calls to find out how much it would cost to have a full back tattoo done of black angel wings. After the third call I was beginning to wonder if it would even be feasible. The next place is Studio Enigma and after I get off the phone with them, I prepare for my 1 o'clock appointment. Anger swirls around me like smoke, nearly tangible. If I were to run my hands through it, it would dissipate only to reform again on the other side. Revenge is the only thought on my mind. Once I was called a sweet angel, but now I will be an angel of revenge.

As I open the front door of the building, I am hit by rain that is slanting into the building. Having known it was raining, I was prepared and opening my umbrella, I look up at the dark skies just as lightning flashes across the tops of buildings in the distance. Although it is the middle of the day, you cannot tell with the deep grey clouds and heavy rain. It was no brighter than dusk all around me and my mood reflected the weather. The rain splashes beneath the edge of my umbrella, replacing the tears threatening to form. I am suddenly not sure if it was the weather affecting my mood or my mood affecting the weather, as it was not raining before I read the article. I look down at my hand, now bandaged, remembering how I felt when I read the paper and how I punched the coffee table leaving no damage to the solid wood but cracking my knuckles open. Anger burns deep inside me and another crack of lightening erupts, closer this time. Tears of frustration finally stream down my face. I cannot believe he did it again before I could stop him. I was determined to get him now. I failed that woman but I **will not** fail again. I want to scream but instead I eat down the anger and hatred, storing it in the box I will open when I have him. Waiting… That is the hardest part, but I know that when I finally have him I can unleash all that pain and hatred and finally get my revenge. On my way to the tattoo parlor, I stop at the corner store to use the ATM. Taking out the money I need plus a little extra for a tip, I head back out into the weather's manifestation of my mood. The place is about six blocks from my apartment building and originally I planned to take a bus but decided I needs to walk off my foul mood before I arrive. At first my thoughts were anchored on the article in the paper with deep waves of anger beating at me but about halfway there I found myself thinking about the previous night. Slowly, the anger recedes and is replaced first with confusion and uncertainty, followed by joy and happiness. When this is all over, I will tell Dean I love him.

The walk is long and I am a little winded from moving against the forces of the storm, but by the time I step in the door, I am feeling much calmer. The rage that filled me is now safely stored away and I am able to give a big smile to the woman at the counter. I remove my soaked jacket, hanging it and the umbrella on some hooks near the door and walk over to the woman.

Giving her my name, she looks in her book and tells me the price. She takes the cash, putting it in the register and then shows me through a door to the back where the man that will be doing my tattoo stands.

He extends a hand and which I shake while we exchange pleasantries and then he hands me a form to read over and sign. It's a basic consent form saying I know what I am getting into and that I am free of any disease and what-not. I initial each of the sections, sign at the bottom and hand the clipboard back to him.

He asks to verify what I want done and he has me turn around so he can get an idea of what he needs to do. After a few moments he asks if I would mind if he free hand draws the wings on.

Knowing I can change my mind if I do not like his drawing, I agree. He tells me I will need to remove my shirt for it and I cringe inside for a moment. I knew I would have to do it, but now that it is real I am uncomfortable with the idea.

He says I can leave my bra on but will need to leave it unhooked in the back and gives me a white medical type towel to cover myself with. He points me to what looks like a massage chair tilted slightly forward and asks me to sit facing the chair and give him a call when I am ready, and then he closes off the area with a couple folding screens.

When he returns, he tells me to relax into it and lean my head forward so he can draw the design. I feel the tip of the Sharpie marker drawing lines on my back as he works in silence.

I had told him before he started that I want traditional bird-like angel wings but in black instead of white. It did not take him long to draw the outlines and when I look in the mirror, I am impressed. The wings look like they were truly coming out of my flesh and folded in against my back.

After approving, he brings me back to the chair where he prepares me for the pain by doing a small line at first. When I do not complain, he starts the long task. He works the outlines first, and then starts to add the shading near the tops.

After nearly three hours, he needs to take a break. I agreed, feeling my blood sugar was a little low, and accept the bottle of Dew he hands me. Carefully I sit up, holding the towel in place, and drink the soda. As I move, my back feels like it is covered in a giant rug burn. The stinging and tingling bring back memories that I immediately shake off.

When he asks how I am doing I reply with "I've felt worse."

He decides to leave the conversation at that and tells me he needs a smoke and will be right back.

I nod and take another gulp of the soda as he walks out the back door, leaving it propped a bit. Looking through the crack I see the rain has stopped and the sun was attempting to peek through the dense clouds. A cool breeze flows into the room and I turn my back to it feeling it cool the burning sensation.

When he returns, he sprays my back down and wipes it off so that he can see where he left off. After a couple more hours of work, he wipes my back down one last time and tells me to go look in the mirror, handing me a large hand mirror.

I walk over and when I see the wings, I nearly break down into tears. The guy was truly an artist! I noticed he added light shading around them to add depth, and where they brushed across the upper curve of my butt, there was deeper shading making them appear to hover over my skin. I thank him and tell him I love them and then he bandages my back up before putting the screens back so I can carefully put my shirt back on. I tuck my bra into my purse as I pull out my wallet and as I come around the screen, I give him a large tip and a heartfelt thank you.

He then gives me a pamphlet with instructions for care of the new tattoo, as well as a sample size tube of a cream to put on it after the first forty-eight hours.

I put them in my purse, go out the main door and say good-bye to the lady before grabbing my coat and umbrella and heading home. The walk home, although dryer, was just as uncomfortable, only now I was in serious discomfort. After getting back to my apartment I take off my shirt and call Dean's cell to leave him a message asking if he can come over after his shift. I then head into the kitchen, do a double shot of Captain Morgan's and go to my bedroom where I lay on my stomach on my bed and I quickly fall asleep.

I wake with a start, causing pain to fill my entire back. At first I am not sure what woke me, but then I hear the knock again.

I rush to the door after seeing the time on my clock, yelling "COMING" as I throw my shirt back on.

After checking through the peephole, I open the door for Dean and before he can get a hold of me for a hug, I jump back and say "I've got a surprise to show you" as I lock up the door.

He gets a concerned expression on his face as he follows me into the bedroom, where I turn away from him and take my shirt off.

I hear his gasp and worry he does not approve but when I turn around, I am surprised to see a little irritation on his face.

"Why didn't you tell me you were going to get that done!" he exclaims.

Anger takes over and I start to yell at him about how he doesn't own me and it's my body, when suddenly he grabs my arms, pulling me close and kisses me.

He then apologizes and explains that he would love to have been there when I had it done and that was all he meant by it.

I give him an OHHH face and then kiss him, giving him an apology of my own for over-reacting.

Dean then turns me back around to get a closer look and offers to clean it and put ointment on it. I know that if I do not let him, I will hurt his feelings so I agree, and besides it was burning really bad. He turns me back around and with a big grin on his face he starts to remove my pants.

"What are you doing?" I ask and with a devilish grin he tells me "with such a large tattoo we will need to go in the shower to clean it properly."

I cannot help but laugh and taking him by the hand, I lead him into the bathroom, removing his shirt as he shuts the door with his foot. I guess he forgives me.

Chapter 11

As Dean heads home to prepare for his training expedition, I walk him out. At the elevator doors, I cuddle him and he gives me a big kiss while we say our good-byes. I know he will only be gone a few days, but I will miss him. After he gets on the elevator, I go back and get my shoes on before locking up the apartment. I give him enough time to be out of the building before I go down to Betty to borrow her car for the weekend. I spend some time chatting with her and she tells me how much she likes 'that nice boy' I am seeing and how she hopes we 'do the right thing.' After a short time I head back up to my apartment and grab my list of addresses to check out. Looking at the first address, I head to the site. It is a two and a half hour drive once outside the city limits and in a very secluded country setting. As I drive down the country roads I cannot help but be awed by the beauty surrounding me. Tall trees replace the stone and metal structures of my everyday life, grass and flowers replace the cement and blacktop. For a few moments, I forget why I am really out here and wonder what would happen if I decide to just take a hike instead. I begin to pull off the side of the road and then remember the newspaper article, which jars me back on track and continue the last few miles to the site. The first site has a SOLD sign over the For Sale sign, so I continue down to the next place on the list which is not that far away.

I nearly drive by the road at first, the sign at the end is made of wood and the paint has faded and chipped with neglect but the numbers at the top are raised up and gray so I know this is the place. As I drive down long twisted overgrown dead end road, there is an old rusted chain across it spanning between two trees and I notice the trees have started to grow over the chain. A faded 'Do Not Enter' sign dangles by one corner slightly off center on the chain and squeaks in the slight breeze. I drive back down the dead end, taking a right on the main road and then go about a quarter mile down to a Scenic Pull-off and park my car. I put on my hiking boots, grab my camera and hiking stick and walk back to the dead end and down to the abandoned drive. I gently walk up to the sign careful not to disturb the weeds and looks over the chain. At first I am concerned by the trees growth but then I notice the chain is actually connected behind the dangling sign with an old key padlock. Pulling rubber gloves from my fanny pack, I put them on and examine the lock. The key opening is rusted and most likely has not been used in a very long time, which is a good sign. Gently stepping over the knee high chain, I examine the roadway just beyond the barrier. It appears to be an old gravel drive but it is overgrown and filled with weeds which means once I drive on it, it will be noticeable. I walk down the road and make notes of the overgrown trees and shrubs along the way; it is obvious nobody has driven down here in a very long time. At the end of the quarter mile long road sits an old Baroque style church. Its placement deep in the woods and far from the main road will make it an excellent site for my plans. Standing at the road's end, I take in the full scene. The paint on the sign in front is worn and nearly impossible to read. 'P tsv le Lut an Chur' The sale ad stated it is an old abandoned church on five acres of land, but did not give the name of the church and I could not help but wonder why.

Walking up to the old church, I touch the stones; they are cold, yet there seemed to be a pulse to them, or perhaps that was my own pulse I am feeling. With my gloved hand, I try the front door to find it unlocked. Stepping inside I am amazed by what lays before me. The front entry with its stone archway and broad nave is welcoming and still intact and the stained glass in the narrow windows on either side seemed to shimmer even though there was no sunlight hitting them and they are coated in years of dust. After calling out a "Hello?" with no response, I step back outside and decide to walk the perimeter first. I want to be sure there are no signs of others using the building, from the outside before possibly getting caught inside. Walking around to the right, I take in the beautiful architecture and wonder why anyone would just leave something like this to be forgotten. Upon reaching the other side where the outer wall had caved in, I realize why. The description stated that there was damage due to lightening. I guess so. I stop and look inside and am awe struck by the high ceiling with what was left of a spectacular trompe l'oeil of angels descending from the clouds painted upon it. Stepping over the rubble of the wall, I enter the church and my breath is taken away by the perfectness of it. I look over the rows of pews and see that the ones farther from the opening are still in good condition. As I walk down the center of the isle, I focus on the alter at the front end of the church. I find it odd that the sermons were held at the front instead of the back of the church and wonder if that has something to do with it being decommissioned, or perhaps it was just the big gaping hole in the side of the church. Although long stripped of fineries and positioned oddly, it is the perfect stage for what I plan to accomplish, directly below the angels that are still in pristine condition on the ceiling. For a moment, I consider the religious ramifications of what I am planning to do in this old church, but then I realize it is actually the perfect place for an avenging angel to take out her wrath upon a sinner. The church and I hold many commonalities. Like the church I have been battered. We have both been broken and left behind, but I shall bring this church back to life by using it to rid the world of evil. Upon reaching the alter, I stand upon it; there is a podium on one side and above, there is a large eye-hook where possibly once a chandelier hung. In my mind I could vision the chain hanging down, my tools on the podium. It was perfect. Looking around the entire church, my heart stops for a moment when I realize it is not as overgrown as I expected it to be. Quickly, I scour the entire church for signs of inhabitants, but there is nothing. I expected to find something, even if it was just litter left by a squatter, but there was none. Looking around outside the church, I find the same thing. It is as if the church was forgotten and left to rot away, or perhaps something happened here and it was purposely abandoned and hidden away.

As I take a second trip around the perimeter of the grounds, I find a path heading away from the clearing on the left side near the far back. Carefully pulling back the branches of an overgrown honeysuckle, I expose an old stone path. Curiosity drives me to follow the path, so I move back several branches to head down it. A way down the path, I come across a small overgrown cemetery, filled with cracked and tipped over headstones. Ivy and weeds cover the ground like a shroud, and on the far end I can see the path picks back up. Carefully making my way through the forgotten cemetery, I continue following the path to see where it ends. Surprisingly, I find it has circled back around and comes out just up the road from where I parked my car at an old abandoned farmhouse. Excitement fills me as I realize I found the perfect escape route, as well as a place to hide my own vehicle on that night. I look around the farmhouse and check out the old barn. Although brittle, the doors still open and the clearing within is large enough for me to hide a car inside. I will not be using Betty's car though because if I get caught, I do not want it to come back on an innocent woman. I walk the path back to the church, checking for anything in the ground that could make my escape treacherous. As I slowly move along, I remove any sharp stones and twigs and also make a drawing in my notebook with the layout of the cemetery, as well as the safest path through it. I fill my notebook with sketches and plans and by the time I return to the church clearing, I have used a dozen or so pages on the farmhouse and path alone. Now I walk back to the church and decide to put out a few items to help see if there are visitors that just clean up really well after themselves. First, I place a piece of paper near the top of the front door between it and the jamb so that if someone opens it the paper will fall out but not even be noticed. I then place a twenty dollar bill under one of the narrow windows slightly tucked between two stones so it would not easily blow away and looks like someone stashed it there for safe keeping. I head out to the podium and scatter a thin layer of dirt on the ground to show footprints. I do the same near the crumbled wall but do not count on it producing anything, as the dirt could be blown or washed away there. After placing a few more items around, I walk back to my car via the road while examining it better. As I arrive at my car, the sun is preparing to set and I feel like I may have lucked out and found the perfect location. All of my needs are met, and as an added bonus I have a place to hide my vehicle and a secret passage out. Excitedly I head home, the trip seemingly shorter with all the thoughts running through my head.

I have just enough time when I get home to change and make it to work with only a few minutes before my shift begins. It is the same old story at the bar, but tonight nothing can touch me, my thoughts focused on my findings. I go through my usual routine, waiting on customers, fending off drunks and finishing the evening by cleaning the place up. On my walk home, I think about the church and the old farmhouse some more. Something is bothering me, but I cannot put my finger on it. I decide to look into the property, see if it is for sale or if someone owns it as well as find out a little about its history. If it is for sale, I do not want to count on it as my escape route because someone may purchase it and start working on the place, but I did not see any "For Sale" signs anywhere near the place, so I am hopeful. That may also change my decision to use the church as well, seeing as it is so close. When I get back to my apartment, I make a note to go to the library and check into it. While at my desk, I find a message from Dean on the answering machine.

He called to tell me he made it there okay and was crazy busy the first few hours. He also mentioned knowing I was at work and wishing he could have talked to me because he misses me.

I look at the time of his message and realize he missed me by less than half an hour and decided he will probably be asleep by now, so I will return his call in the morning. After taking a quick shower, suffering the cooler temperature water since the hot water irritates my new tattoo; I wish Dean was around to put the ointment on my back. After a lot of stretching and straining, I finally decide to slather some of the ointment on some plastic wrap, and holding both ends like a towel, I use that to spread the cream over my back. Wired from work and my findings, I decide to watch some television with my top off to allow the cream to absorb into my skin. Wearing nothing but my pajama bottoms, I grab a chair from the kitchen and head to the living room. With the chair facing backwards I sit down on it and rest my arms on the top of the backrest, leaning my chin on my arm. Using the remote, I flip through the channels until I find something that looks interesting. An hour later, I head to my room, carefully put on my pajama top and head to sleep. Normally I don't wear them but with the new tattoo I wanted something protecting me when I toss and turn. And that I do, until sleep finally takes over, leaving me in my own private hell of nightmares.

It is Sunday morning and I wake early for my day, which includes a trip out to the old church. I am extremely tired after a restless night's sleep. Between the irritation from my tattoo and the nightmares, I spent a lot of time tossing and little time actually sleeping. First thing I did was put on a full pot of coffee and while drinking a couple cups, I fill my carafe with hot water to get it pre-warmed and then I give Dean a call. I hope that he will be available to chat but instead I get his voicemail. Disappointed, I leave a message and add how much I am missing him. After hanging up, I go back into the kitchen and fry up an egg, making toast at the same time. After cooking the egg over-hard, I slap on a slice of cheese and turn off the burner while retrieving my toast. Throwing it all together, I sit down with yet another cup of coffee and my breakfast sandwich and think about how to go about my day. I plan to hit the library at some point and look into the property more, but it is closed today. So I decide to take another walking inspection to look for any evidence of visitors. After putting the rest of the pot into the carafe with a little creamer, I make up a peanut butter and jelly sandwich and grab an apple and my travel coffee mug, and I am off. I decide to park at the farm after seeing it's been untouched since I was last there. To be on the safe side, I put a note in the window saying I am a hiker and just parked here to keep my car safe. I then head down the path to the old cemetery with my hair bundled up and tucked in a hat and my gloves on. As I follow the path through it, I walk slowly, removing any branches and sharp rocks that are along the path I missed before, as well as moving any prickly branches that have grown toward it. I am very careful to not break any of the branches as I move them, trying to intertwine them with other foliage as naturally as possible. When I am satisfied with the safeness of the path, I head to the church. First, I look around outside, there appears to be no new footprints, and the mud that built up near the entrance of the broken wall, from the rain they received here last night looks unmarred by human or animals. Carefully, I avoid the mud myself and head around to the front. I check the door and am pleased when I find my tiny piece of paper falling down upon opening it. I tuck the paper into my pocket and look around inside. I find that the dust and dirt has still been untouched as well as all the items I left around. I am pleased by this but know not to get my hopes up quite yet, since it was only a night. Just because it was untouched this weekend, it does not mean it will still be untouched in a couple weeks. I look around some more and leave more little markers for when I return again. After I am satisfied, I head out the front door, returning my paper scrap and head down the road. Carefully, I examine the chain and lock; both seem untouched. Finally, I take the main road back to my car, there I eat my lunch and then look around the farm a little. I notice the cobwebs and overgrown yards, the windows are crudely boarded up yet nobody has attempted to enter the house. The place is truly abandoned and satisfied, head home.

As I am pulling into the lot behind the building, my cell phone rings. I answer and it's Dean; he tells me he called the house first but no answer.

I tell him I was out running errands and just got home. Grabbing the bag with my leftovers from lunch in one hand and my cell phone propped between my other shoulder and ear, I lock up the car and head into the building. I wave as I get buzzed in the back door and head up to my apartment.

Meanwhile, Dean tells me about the training so far and how exhausted he is already and that he's extremely glad it's almost over.

"It's gonna kill me" he exclaims and I tell him "I sure hope not! Because then who will watch movies with me?"

This gets a laugh out of him and he thanks me, telling me he needed something to lighten the mood. After I get to my apartment, I lay down on my stomach on the couch and Dean and I talk for nearly half an hour when I hear a horn, or siren or some other really loud obnoxious sound on his end.

He sighs heavily and tells me he needs to go back to training.

"Already? What happened to time to socialize?" I ask in shock, and he tells me they changed the schedule and was glad I could not come because I would have been bored out of my mind, waiting for him to be free.

I wish him luck and blow him a kiss over the phone and he returns the favor before saying good-bye and "See you tomorrow", and then hanging up.

My stomach grumbles at me and I realize it's past dinner time, so I head into the kitchen and heat up a Hungry Man dinner. I've been finding myself eating them more and more since I started working out. I used to eat the much smaller dinners but I have had much more of an appetite now. I bring my food and a bottle of Pepsi into the living room and sit down, turning on the television. There's a "Fast and Furious" marathon on so, I settle in and start eating. After getting my Vin Diesel fix and filling my belly with fried chicken, I clean up my trash and pop in the shower quick before heading to bed. I want to get up early tomorrow, do my work out, hit the library and hopefully be at Dean's about the time he will be getting home.

Heading to the gym, I grab some extra change so that I can get one of the lockers with the locks on it instead of my usual cubby. Before leaving, I tucked my notebook in my gym bag so that I could head straight from the gym to the library a couple blocks away. I knew I would not have time to run home after my workout, get to the library and back home before going to see Dean, so I decided to cut out some of the traveling. Besides, going to the library sweaty and smelly might keep away unwanted company and allow me the privacy I need. I get to the gym and put in a hard workout, seeing as I have been missing them on occasion and need to make up for lost time. I also hit the punching bag for a bit, practicing the moves I learned from a workout video I rented. I am lucky enough to have the boxing instructor walk by and offer me a couple free tidbits of advice, because he does not want to see me injure myself. After correcting my stance and hand positions, I find it to go a lot more smoothly and actually enjoy this workout more than the weights and machines. When I am winded enough, I head to the showers and seeing nobody in there, hop in long enough to rinse off the excess sweat before drying and dressing. Grabbing my bag, I head to the library.

I walk in and take the long way around to the computers. First I hit the self--h Help section and browse a bit before taking a quick trip to the rest rooms and then finally I sit down at the computers. Nobody is present and I had been waiting for the woman who was there to leave. She had just gotten up and walked toward the front of the library and I noticed she was still logged in, so I waited a few moments before she returned. When she did not, I sat at her computer and started using it under her log-in. First, I check several of the realtor sites both local to that area and state-wide but come up with nothing for either the house or the church. I then decide to do a search for "Church" itself and the road name and found Pottsville Lutheran Church. The church is owned by a Pastor Thomas Nichols, but has been left unused for the past eight years. Looking into Pastor Thomas some more, I find out that he used to live at the farm house with his wife but when she died in a horrible accident at the church, he left the church and home and swore never to return. He still owns the property because he will not allow anyone else use or purchase it, but he is basically letting it rot. I am so excited to hear about the state of the property, but I am also curious to see what happened, so I look but cannot find anything more. I decide to check the library near the church as they may have print copies of the newspaper available. After making several notes in my book, I sign out and take the long way out of the library and head home.

Looking at the time, I realize I won't be able to catch Dean at the station if I take a shower, so I give him a call.

He answers on the first ring and tells me he's been waiting all morning for me to call.

I apologize and tell him about my experience at the gym and how I lost track of time with my new-found favorite exercise.

He laughs and asks if I have showered yet, I tell him no and that I called for that exact reason.

I explain that I am a sweaty stinky mess and I can either meet him at the station like that or I can shower and meet him home.

He surprises me by telling me that he does not mind if I am sweaty since he is too; they left right after the final training session without taking showers. He continued with how we can shower together and he can see how my back is healing.

I can tell by his voice that he really misses me, so I agree and tell him I just need to get together an overnight bag and I will meet him there.

Excited by my inviting myself to stay the night at his place, he tells me he cannot wait and blows me a kiss before hanging up.

I quickly tuck away my notebook and repack my gym bag with clean clothes before rushing out the door to meet up with Dean. I get to the station not long after his bus pulls up and he is still waiting to get his bags out of the compartment. He's not looking in my direction, so I take the opportunity to sneak up behind him and wrap my arms around his waist. Looking down he immediately recognizes my wrists and pulls me around into a big hug, being careful of my tattoo. After he gets his bag, we head to his car parked in the secured lot and head back to his place to play catch up. On the way, he talks non-stop about the hell he went through at training but how it is worth it because it makes him a better fireman. As soon as we arrive at his apartment, he whisks me off to the bathroom where we take a long shower together before heading off to his room.

Chapter 12

It has been a week since I last visited the church, and I decide it is time to return and see if there has been any activity. Things between Dean and I have been going really well, but I can feel this itch deep in my soul; it is calling to me and reminding me I have a task to complete. Even though a part of me wants to forget about it all and just move on with my life with Dean, another part of me screams for revenge.

Borrowing the car from Betty yet again, I get some supplies together just after Dean leaves for work and I head out. He is working a double and I have the night off, so it is the perfect time to go check on my site. Messenger bag over one shoulder, lunch bag in the other, I head down to the car and start my journey. I make a pit stop about halfway there, at a garage sale. I was drawn to it after seeing a large old mirror propped up against the end of a folding table. Thinking it would go well with my plans, I decide to buy it and carefully load it into the back of my car. I get back on the road and make my way to the old house, where I park in the barn. Pulling the mirror out and hiding it behind some old bales, of hay I walk out and carefully close the door, hiding the car away behind me. Taking the path through the cemetery, I look for any new debris that may have fallen since my last visit. I also find that some of my rearranging from last time did not take, so I have to fix the briars again.

When I get to the church, I take a walk of the perimeter first and then I do an interior check. I can see it's still in the same condition it was in last time, all of my markers are still in place and I do not see any signs of visitors. Even though it is going to be a couple more weeks before I return for the final time, I cannot help but begin preparations of the site. I go around clearing up the main area and getting props into place. I spend several hours shuffling things around before I head back to the car. Things are coming together so perfectly and I am super excited, planning one more trip, a few nights before my final visit, to ensure the security.

After I finish up at the church and am satisfied with the path, I take a drive to the local library, hoping they keep all old newspaper articles. I wander in and the place is nearly empty except for an elderly man sitting behind a very large desk. I would have not even noticed him but for the fact that his full head of white hair moves as I enter.

As I walk toward the desk, he groggily sits up and gives me a friendly welcome. He points out that I must be an "out-o-towner" because he does not recognize me, and I laugh and tell him I'm up from the city to do some hiking and was curious about the area.

I played it up that I enjoy looking into the history of an area that I intend to hike in. With a laugh, I joke that I do not want to run into any unhappy ghosts or anything like that.

This was the perfect thing to say because it prompts him to warn me not to visit the old church if I'm "afeard of ghosts."

I cannot help but show interest and ask him to tell me more about it.

He says I may want to grab a seat and he will tell me all about it, since he was there when it all started all those many years ago.

*** The Librarian's Tale in his words ***

It was nineteen years ago, the church was in its fullest glory and the parishioners all loved the services. The entire community went out there every Sunday to hear Pastor Thomas 'cus he always knew what to say to alls us. He and his wife had been married for several years but never had any children. Some folks talked but most of us believed there was a higher purpose to it. They devoted their life to that there church and after every service, his wife Mary... Yup that really was her name.... Mary would make up a dinner for all the townsfolk that were in need. She'd make up a big ol' ham or turkey, smashed potatoes with lots a butter and a sprinkling of garlic and a big bowl of hand cut off the cob sweet corn. Sometimes, it'd be a big pot of stew with veggies fresh out her garden or a disk of baked pasta. There would also be a basket of fresh rolls she would bake up that morning before coming in. Those were the best meals I ever ate, let me tell you. She took care of her flock she did, we were all her children she would say. But I digress... The night Mrs. Mary died, Pastor Thomas died as well but on the inside [he points to his chest to emphasize this.] *We all saw his heart shattering right there on his face and knew that was the end of our church. HAH! But now I am getting too far ahead! So anyway, that morning started same as every other Sunday morning. Father Thomas stood up at the front and started talking about war, since that was what was all over the news right now, and Mrs. Mary stood at the back where she always stood, a proud look on her face as she listened to her husband. As always she stood at the back, her rosary wrapped around her left hand, her bible in her right pressed up against her chest, and that look of adoration and happiness on her face. There was a storm raging outside but none of us noticed it much over the organ playing in the background and the Pastor emphatically talking about how God believes war is wrong. He just slammed his hand down on the podium when there was a loud crack followed by an ear piercing crashing from behind us. We all turned as one and saw that the back of the church was all crumbled down right where Mary was standing and she w'ant there anymore. We all sat there in shock, partially at the pile of stone, partially at the rain suddenly coming in where there was once a wall, partially because the good woman wasn't there no more. Pastor Thomas went rushing down the aisle, screaming her name over and over. I tell ya, I spoke ta many of those there that day and they all say they could hear the Pastor's faith slip with every time he called her name and there was no answer. When he got back there, he started pushing those stones out o' the way like they were pillows and quickly we saw the blood on his hands where the jagged edges were tearing them apart. This was what finally snapped us out o' our shock and all of us men got over there and helped him, even a few of the lady folk got in on the diggin. Finally we found her, though you'd not been able to recognize what was left of her. Poor Thomas, he leaned down over her crumpled body and let out a cry that to this day haunts ever one of our souls. He cursed God for what he did and swore he'd not have a lick to do with him ever again. When the ambulance arrived and took her away, he just turned toward the church and all of us and said that the church is closed from this day on and that he does not want to see anyone come near this place ever again.*

(Here the man pauses and looks down at his hands clasped in his lap. The expression on his face is one of loss. Although long ago, I could see it was still fresh in his heart. When he looks up, there are tears threatening to escape his eyes and he clears his throat a couple times before continuing.)

They took Mrs. Mary's body from us and Thomas followed behind in his old Impala. Now I don't call him Pastor no mo' 'cause he lost his faith when that wall came down. She is buried in the back yard of their old farmhouse; as he refused to put her in the church cemetery. He then shut it all up from the world, refusing to sell it to this day but not letting anyone out there. For many a year, he sat on the front porch of that ol house and stared up at the sky.

Occasionally, if you drove past you could see him swearing at the stars or hanging his head in sadness. Eventually, he ended up in one of those homes, you know the ones for those people that just can't deal with life no more? Well, he has himself a living will and in that will it states that the church, cemetery and that old house are not to be touched by anyone. They are all that's left of his Mary, which is why he's not had that church leveled, but he refuses to ever go back there and ya know what? I don't blame him one bit. He's got the money to cover the taxes for many more years still so the gov—n-mint won't be bothering with it for a while. He's planning to just let that place rot away, I think. Now many are upset about that, be sure of it, but we will abide by his wishes cus some of us know the pain he still feels to this day. So now you are probably wondering what I mean by angry spirits aren't ya? Well it's believed that if you go out to the old farmhouse on the third o' May you will see Mrs. Mary's spirit carrying the baskets of food to the church same as she did that day, but when she gets there and sees the wall all torn down, her spirit goes all crazy like...Dark and angry. Well's least that's what they say, I've not seen it myself. They say that's the reason why Thomas lost it completely though. That he saw her out there raging and screaming. Never really know though, will we? He won't talk to anyone these days and ain't nobody willin to go out there and find out themselves.
******

With that, he shakes his head and then looks down for a bit. Looking down at this frail old man, a deep sadness etched in his old weary face, I feel like I might be interrupting his personal thoughts. I quietly head to the back of the library where the newspapers and such are and start looking for articles. What I find pretty much collaborates with what the librarian told me, although the papers left out some of the details. After a time, I decide to head home, so I give the man at the desk a cheerful thank you and goodbye and excitedly get in the car. The ride seems shorter this time, as my thoughts are filled with planning. First thing I will need however, is my own car before I can complete my task. When I get back to my apartment, I start scouring the internet for possibilities.

As I am looking there is a knock at the front door and I realize I planned to make dinner for Dean and I tonight.

With an "Oh crap", I run to the door and check it is him before opening.

As always I am greeted with a big smile and hug, and even after admitting I was caught up in searching for a car and forgot to make dinner, he still smiles.

Without a negative word, Dean suggests delivery and I feel an urge to tell him how much I care about him but stuff it down instead.

I can't feel those feelings until all the dark ones are banished. Instead, I give him a big kiss and suggest pizza.

He counters with calzones and I jump on the band wagon without hesitation.

I always forget we can get them for delivery, and I much prefer them to the richly sauced and highly greasy pizza. While I make the call to the pizza place,

Dean starts looking at the numerous pages I have open with car ads. "I notice a trend" he says as I walk into the room "You seem to have a thing for the old muscle cars. You're not just with me for mine, are you?"

I laugh and tell him it's because my pop used to take me to the car shows all summer long and I always thought those old cars with their curves and shapes are a hundred times more beautiful than these newer ones. There is just something sexy about a car with curves. It is his turn this time to laugh as he just shakes his head. We sit down and look some more, but I just cannot find the car I am looking for, so eventually I close the laptop and cuddle up to Dean. He's been watching some sports game on the television while occasionally peeking at whatever new car I am squealing over and now he puts his arm around me and places a kiss on the top of my head. Soon after, the food arrives and I grumble as he has to get up and answer the door.

We already argued over the fact I was supposed to make dinner, but his old fashioned manliness would not let him allow me to pay for the food.

I finally agree but not without telling him I would make it up to him later. With a big grin on his face, Dean puts in an old movie from my shelf and we eat cuddled together on the couch until it starts getting late and we head off to my room, with him wearing that same big grin.

Over the next couple days, I plan a trip to get out of town for the next week so that I can finalize my plans and get the last few items I need for my revenge. It has been only four months since my attack, although it feels like it was much longer. I am feeling an overwhelming need for closure, so that I can finally start my life as it should be. I have the excuse of having found the perfect car but that it is in Modesto, California so I will have to take the train there and drive the new car home.

Dean asks why I do not fly there, as it will be quicker and possibly even cheaper but I gently remind him of my extreme fear of flying, although that is only partially it.

I know that if I fly, the trip would be shortened enough he might be able to pull off getting time off to go. This way, I do not have to worry about hurting his feelings by telling him I want to go alone. I am however genuinely excited about the car as it is a 1972 Corvette Stingray in a deep metallic purple, my dream car. The owner passed away and the family did not want to keep it any longer, so they put it up for sale. I found it on the internet and decided I just **have** to have it, so I offered the family a deal and they took it. I transferred them the money and they transferred the title to my name and said it would be ready when I get there. I was able to do the registration online, so I have the new plates in hand when I get there. I want to be sure the car is completely legal for my cross-country supply run home. I had come to the realization that if I got all of my supplies locally, I increase my chances of being caught so I am going to spread my shopping trip out across the country, only buying a couple items in each state as I pass through. It is the middle of summer, so I borrow a one man tent from Dean and plan to camp at state parks along the way home to save on hotel costs, but it also minimizes my chances of being seen and or remembered and thus possibly tied to anything.

The morning I leave, Dean takes me to the station. I only have a hiking pack with my clothes and necessities and strapped to it are the tent and a sleeping bag.

Dean tells me I am insane to do something like this but that he also envies me for taking a chance and doing something wild and care-free.

I give him a reassuring hug and kiss and tell him it's something I need to do, that I cannot spend my whole life afraid and locked away and he tells me that he understands my reasons but that does not mean he has to like them.

Placing my bag between my feet, ticket in hand, we stand there in silence waiting for my train to arrive. Dean is standing behind me, his arms wrapped possessively around my waist. I have allowed myself to melt into him, trying to give him the comfort and reassurance he needs with my body, since words did not work. He starts rubbing his hands slowly up and down my arms and I feel a pang of guilt for needing to leave, but it is only for a week, maybe less depending on my travel time getting home. If I can drive longer distances and sleep shorter, then I might be able to get home sooner. We discussed all of this last night, but it seems he listened but did not hear.

Dean and I spent several hours discussing my trip, yet again this morning, and we even had our first fight over it. It nearly ended with me breaking it off since he was being so stubborn, but eventually he gave in and accepted it or so I thought. Instead, he had just let me believe he did. Now as we stand here, I can feel he has not accepted it at all. I can feel it in the tenseness of his muscles and by the way he is nervously rubbing my arms.

I try one last time to tell him I will be fine and he just says "I know" in that lost and dejected tone he has been using all morning.

I decide I will deal with it when I get home, but right now I just need to get the car and the items for my plan. Who knows, if I get caught or if Dean figures out what I am doing, I might just lose him anyway. It was foolish of me to even get into a relationship before completing my plan. It is not my fault though that Dean has a white knight complex and managed to sweep me off my feet however. I was so caught up in my emotions; I nearly missed the announcement for my train. I think Dean took it as hesitation about leaving and relaxed a little until I quickly grabbed my bag, his hand and rushed toward the train.

When we approach the platforms edge, he pulls me into his arms and kisses me with such emotion, I have a brief flash of doubt and when he pulls back he says "I love you, come back to me" and quickly pushes me onto the train, rushing off before I can respond.

I stand there in the doorway, speechless for several moments before a man asked to see my ticket.

Handing him the ticket, he shows me the direction to my seat and I wander down the aisle, lost in a whirl-wind of emotion. I brought some books to read on the trip but often I just find myself staring out the window, thinking where I am going and what I am going to do once I finish my task. I just hope Dean survives through it all untouched and that one day I can tell him I feel the same way.

Chapter 13

Although it is an extremely long ride, Dean calls me several times while I am on the train, to help alleviate the boredom. His first call, however, was to be sure we are still okay. After that we talked about everything but me being on the road. It was as if we truly believe if we didn't talk about it, the problem would go away, but I am never one for skirting the issues.

Finally I blurt out "You know you went away for a while too, I don't see why it's such a big deal!"

Dean went silent and after what seemed like an eternity he just says, "But that is different." As if that explains everything.

Frustrated, I ask, "How? How is it different when you are gone for long periods but when I need to go away it's suddenly the end of the world?"

I get no answer for a while. The silence is eating away at me, I can hear my heart beating in my ears and finally he responds with

"You're right. I have no right to tell you what you can or can't do. I am sorry. As you've made it clear in the past, we are just dating." It is my turn to sigh. Now he has brought up *that* conversation again.

"Dean, you know I can't offer you more right now. I need to finish healing and figure out where I belong now in the grand scheme of things, before I can do that. Besides, we have not even been dating a year; we have not lived together or anything. Please give me time."

He responds with a curt "I know" and "Okay" then he tells me he needs to go get ready for work and hangs up before I even get to say good-bye.

He does not call me back after that, and when I try to call him he does not answer. My train arrives in Modesto nearly three days after I left New York, a day and a half since I last spoke to Dean. It amazes me how long it took to get here, seeing as the trip home is only supposed to take a couple days nonstop. I figure if I sleep for a few hours each day, and do not take too long on my stops, I could definitely be home in less than a week.

I give Dean a call and leave him a message letting him know I arrived okay and that I am waiting for a taxi to take me to the house with my car.

By this point, I figure he needs time to get over it, but that I will still leave him messages with updates on my trip so that it does not add worry to his pain.

When the taxi arrives, I give him the address and make a call to the sellers, letting them know I am on my way over from the train station and will be arriving by cab.

They thank me for the call and tell me they will have the car out and ready to go.

I am so excited, I can't wait to see my new baby and for a moment, I manage to forget the tension with Dean, as well as my task ahead. All I can think of is getting behind the wheel of that car with the wind blowing in the windows and music on the radio.

About twenty minutes later, we pull up in front of the house and there she is, sitting in the driveway. They had just finished washing her and the sun is glistening off the paint like little sparkles. My jaw drops and I let out a low whistle.

The taxi driver asks if that is the car I have been telling him about and I tell him it is. He shares his envy as I hand him the fare plus a nice tip and step out the door. He asks if I need help with my bags and I thank him but let him know it is not necessary.

Then I grab my bags out and close the door. He drives off as I walk up the path, and a middle-aged couple comes out the front door just as I reach it.

The lady extends her hand to me as we near each other and she welcomes and thanks me.

Her husband is holding the keys and asks to see some identification and the paperwork before he hands them over to me.

I completely understand and appreciate his cautiousness and show him my driver's license and the packet I slip from the front pocket of my backpack.

He looks at my license, looks at me, looks at it again and with a big smile hands me it and the keys. I cannot help but squeal with delight as I head to the car and unlock the driver's side door. The key turns smooth and I am impressed by the care the previous owner must have given it. Sliding in, I feel myself immediately settle into the seat and with the door still open, I start her and the engine purrs. With a big grin, I shut her back off and remove the key from the ignition.

Stepping out, I look at them, my excitement written all over my face and the woman says "I'm so glad you're the one that will be taking the car, now at least I know Papa's baby will be in good hands." With that, she shakes my hand again before excusing herself, tears forming in her eyes, and she goes inside.

Her husband offers to help me get the plates and stickers on and I accept with a smile.

He pulls a screwdriver out of his back pocket and holds it up, "I came prepared" and he gives a happy little chuckle.

I cannot help but give him a big smile and he opens the packet I had handed him and pulls out the first plate. Once the car is legal, I pick up my bags from where I left them on the walk and place them in the passenger seat. I turn and shake hands one last time before I slide behind the wheel once again. I need to readjust the seat a little, but once I do, it feels so natural. I have been left alone with the car now and I run my hands over the steering wheel, feeling the leather, softened by years of hands on it. Then I run my hand across the spotless dashboard, feeling the almost snakeskin-like quality of it. I wonder how much of the cleanliness was the owners and how much was the sellers and decide it must be a combination of both, with the excellent shape everything is still in.

Leaning back, I pull out the GARMIN Dean let me borrow, but could not get myself to suction cup it to the windshield so instead I set it in the spotless ashtray. The wife had told me her father would not allow anyone to smoke in the car and she was not joking, the ashtray looked as clean as the day it was made. I type in my home address and after several moments of it trying to connect, it tells me which way to begin my journey home.

Before pulling out, I give Dean a call and leave him a message telling him I have the car and I am on my way home, and that I will call periodically to let him know where I am.

Hanging up, I place my cell on the passenger seat next to my things and put the car in drive. After a short distance on the highway, I realize it is completely silent in the car now that the woman in the GARMIN stopped talking to me and I decide to turn the radio on.

After sifting through numerous stations and not finding anything that catches my attention, I figure I can just throw in one of the CD's I packed when I realize it only has a tape player. I let slip a word I rarely ever use before grumbling and putting on a classical station. It's not what I want to listen to, but it is better than silence.

The car had a full tank of gas when I picked it up, so I do not need to fill up for quite a while. When I finally do need to stop, I find a little note taped on the inside of the gas tank flap. It is faded and worn, but in soft black letters it says "Don't use the cheap stuff!" I giggle and know that it was 'Papa' that left the note. I leave it where I found it, and swipe my credit card for the only time of the trip. I select the highest octane available and fill the tank, giving the nozzle a few shakes before removing it. I am extra careful that not a drop of gas spills onto the car. I figure at this pace I will need to fill the tank five, possibly six times before I even get to Reno. With a heavy sigh I wonder what I was thinking, at approximately fifty dollars a tank, I may run out of money before I even get home and that is without buying anything. With a heavy sigh, I realize I will have to use the credit card a couple times on the trip home after all but only for gas and snacks and only on stops nowhere near where I picked up any of my supplies. Preferably at stations along the route that I would take had I gone directly home. After filling up, I pull into a spot in front of the convenience center and get out, stretching before heading inside.

I walk in and ask the young girl behind the counter if they have any tapes and she points me toward one of the isles. I walk down it and it's full of stationary and scotch tape.

I go back to the counter and clarify that I am looking for 'music tapes' and she stares at me blankly.

"Really? You don't know what a tape is?" I ask her in disbelief.

She just continues to stare at me dumbfounded and I ask if there's anyone working here over thirty.

She calls toward the back for someone named Jim and soon after this man that looks to be in his late thirties, early forties walks out.

"Can I help you Miss?" he asks in a tired tone, and I tell him I am looking for tapes and that the teeny bopper here has no clue what I am talking about.

With a laugh he tells me they do not carry them but that I can find them in a little used music shop just down the street, really cheap.

He writes down the name of the place and simple directions and wishes me a good day before heading back into the storage room.

I walk out, giving the girl a "thanks for nothing" look and hop in the car. I head to the place he recommended and luckily they are open. It's a small shop with lots of records and tapes and as I take it all in, I wish I had more time to browse and more money to spend. I head to the wall marked Rock N' Roll and find a few by bands from my teenage years. I head to the register. When he starts ringing me up, I am pleased to find out all the tapes were on sale and that I just got the ten of them for fifteen dollars. Ecstatic, I head out to the car and pop the first one in. As Pink Floyd's "The Wall" starts playing I cannot help but feel a renewed excitement about this trip.

Before taking the off-ramp to Reno, Nevada, I gas up at one of the throughway stations and put it on my card. Then I continue to Reno, where I visit two stores. The first one is a Gothic style shop and that is where I get my long black hooded robe with hidden pockets and a pair of black Oriental style silk slippers with smooth leather bottoms. While there, I head over to the jewelry counter and find a set of really simple stainless steel finger nails ornamented with a pair of dragons with red gemstone eyes. The nails are about an inch long and taper to a rounded tip. When I try them on, they slip over my fingertips easily and secure snugly around my first knuckle. I look them over and decide they can easily be sharpened, so I add them to my basket. Walking up to the counter, I add some black lipstick and eyeliner to it before setting it down and moving it toward the clerk. He rings it all up and gives me a price. Without saying a word, I hand him the cash, take my change and bag and walk out. Next, I head down the block to a jewelry supply store where I get a package of earring hoops and a package of dagger charms. Again I pay for everything with minimal conversation. As I am heading back to my car, I remember I will also need some red spray paint so I stop at a hardware store just past where I parked, dropping the bags off on the way. After getting the paint, I head out, making a pit stop at McDonalds for a large iced mocha coffee and some cherry pies to tide me over.

After being on the road for almost twelve hours, I decide to stop at Wasatch National Forest in Utah to get a few hours of sleep. The place reminds me of a scene from one of those horror movies as I drove down a dirt road among the old overgrown trees. I keep expecting some axe-swinging maniac to jump onto the roof of my car and take out my windshield or put his axe through the roof, but it does not happen of course. I find a spot set a little off the road, where I pull over and drop my seat back. I close my eyes and listen to the sounds drifting through my partially opened window until sleep overtakes me. Exhaustion having won the battle, I did not dream, and two hours later I am woken up by the sound of the 1812 Overture. At first I wonder if someone pulled up beside me, when I realize it is the ring tone I set for my alarm on my cell phone. Groggily, I blink several times and reached for one of the energy drinks tucked in the foam cooler on the floor in my passenger seat. Downing it, I rub my eyes and look around. It is so quiet and peaceful, and I wish I could truly enjoy it, but I want to get home.

Turning the engine over, I make my way out the same way I came in and get back to the highway, making a note that I need to replace the ice in my cooler and pick up some more drinks. I think about the conversation with Dean again and I cannot help but wonder what I am going to do about him. I know that I love him, that much is certain. My heart flutters every time I hear his voice or see him. I know he loves me as well, he is constantly suggesting we move forward with our relationship, but I am not ready for that yet. I need to finish this task before I can move on in any way in my life.

Sighing heavily, I look around at the only other two cars on the road and wonder what they are doing with their lives. I imagine the man driving the old Pinto is a college professor on his way home from an out of town tavern after a long night of drinking away his frustrations. In the other car is a family. The man is driving and the woman in the passenger seat has her head resting against the window, her eyes closed. In the back I can see a teenager in the same position cradling what I imagine is a younger sibling sleeping. I wonder if they are headed to see family, perhaps a road-trip to an amusement park or something. I smile at the thought of starting my own family and then I shake my head and go back to concentrating on the road.

In one of the towns I stop for gas in, I find a neat little new age store. I decide to get a few things from there, including the incense sticks, a wooden burner for them, a large white candle and a large marble cauldron shaped bowl.

The girl behind the counter says it looks like I'm "fixing to perform a ritual" and I smile and tell her it's a cleansing.

She smiles back and throws in a small white candle as a gift.

I thank her and tuck everything in the bowl, carrying them out to the car and stashing them in the trunk. Noticing an old record store across the street, I decide to go in, in the hopes of getting a couple more tapes. I have listened to the ones I bought a couple times now and could really use something new. As I walk in, I notice a couple of cardboard boxes of tapes next to the counter with '$1 each' written on the side. I riffle through it and find several 80's and early 90's hair bands. With a handful of tapes, I cash out and get back out to the highway. This time, my thoughts do not wander to the future but instead to the past. I think about all the things I could have done with my life if things had been different. I think of what I should have done; gone to college, became an artist, but now that has all been taken from me. Not that I would have ever gone through with it anyway, but at least then it was my choice.

I've only been on the road for nine hours since I stopped to sleep, but I guess the three hour nap was not enough, so I decide to pull over in Colorado Springs to get a few more hours sleep. I am really exhausted by this point and I cannot get my mind around finding a secure location, so instead I pull into one of the truck stops and find myself a secluded spot way in the back away from the noise of the running rigs. I do not dare leave the window open, even the smallest amount, since I do not know how safe the place is. My car has those old locks, the kind with the big end that you pull up, and someone could easily have the door unlocked on me before I know it if I am sound enough asleep. Instead, I roll them completely down allowing the car to fill with fresh air before closing them tight. I make sure both locks are secure then I throw my seat back and fall into a light sleep. I wake about thirty minutes before my alarm was set to go off by a loud noise. Startled I look around but I do not see anything. Moments later there is another loud bang off to my left. Not knowing what it is and not wanting to find, out I quickly flip my seat back up and take off. My heart is racing as I focus on the parking lot, lights off. I want to attract as little attention as possible to myself, so that who or whatever was making that horribly loud noise would not notice me. As I turn onto the road, I flip my lights on and tear out of there toward the highway, spraying small stones in my wake.

As I pull onto the on-ramp, I reach over and grab an energy drink, downing it before I even hit the end of the merge. Even though I was running on adrenaline, I knew I was going to crash real soon and wanted to thwart the reaction before it happens. It is late at night, so it is dark. But it is early enough that there is still traffic on the road. I fall in among a small group of cars and follow their speed, going about eight to ten miles per hour over the speed limit. As we drive along, I get glimpses of the scenery but at night it is difficult to make out details, it is mostly black silhouettes against a deep blue backdrop. I watch the cars around me and occasionally one will exit and another will join up with us.

After a couple hours, I make a pit stop for some gas and to refill my cooler and grab a snack. After grabbing a box of Twinkies, some Twizzlers and the drinks I need, I head to the counter. As I am standing there, I see some NoDoz and throw a box of it in with my supplies.

The young guy behind the counter looks at me as he pulls the NoDoz out of my basket and comments on how I should probably get some sleep instead of using this stuff.

I thank him for his advice and tell him I just do not have the time for that right now though. After handing him the cash for the gas and my goods, I head out to the car and look in the rear-view mirror. No wonder he was concerned, my eyes are bloodshot and there are dark circles around them. I had not realized how tired I must be and promised to get a little more sleep at my next stop. For now however I need to get as far as I can before my next break.

It has been about thirteen hours since I last slept. I pull in to the Mark Twain National Forest in Missouri, as my body starts shutting down. It decided it finally needs more than two or three hours sleep at a time to continue the journey, so I pull into the park and set up my tent, cuddling up in my sleeping bag. Six hours later, I wake and it's pitch black outside. I look at my clock and it is nearly three in the morning. With Memphis being about five hours away, I realize I should get on the road and get to my next supply run. Carefully I pack the tent back up and stretch. It was not a full night of sleep but it was enough to leave me refreshed and ready to go. Deciding to take a moment to enjoy the peacefulness of the forest, I lean against my hood and eat a pre-made ham and cheese sandwich I picked up at the last stop. The lettuce and tomato are soggy and wilted but it still tastes good, and it is the first real thing I have eaten in almost a day. I decided I could no longer live off sugar and caffeine, and needed to occasionally have something healthy to eat, so I stocked up on some sandwiches and fruit cups at my last stop. As I finish the sandwich and pull out one of the fruit cups, I realize I have nothing to eat it with. Laughing I search around in the bags for something that might work and find a wooden stirrer from a coffee I had yesterday. The stick was still clean since I decided to drink the coffee black, so I used it to skewer the fruit bits. It worked, although I managed to drop a piece of peach down the front of my shirt. With a frustrated sigh, I reach into the car again and pull out a wet wipe from the container on the passenger seat and wipe up the juice the best I can. I finish off the fruit, dumping the juice next to a nearby tree and throw all the garbage into the bag I am keeping on the passenger side floor.

I look around to be sure I didn't drop anything, other than the peach chunk, and get in the car and back on the road. I am feeling refreshed and after eating some healthy food, my mind is actually clear. With a smile on my face, I am back on the road and about halfway to my next stop, I see a sign for a junkyard. I remember I need a winch and some chain for the crucial part of my plan so I take the exit on the sign and follow the road back to a large yard full of all sorts of old cars and trucks. I walk in the dilapidated old building through a door that doesn't look like it can even close and up to the folding table being used as a front desk.

The old guy behind the counter asks "Ken ah hep ya?" in a thick southern drawl, as he pulls on the straps of his overalls.

I tell him what I need and he points me to a section behind the building where there are assorted winches off old trucks. I try and lift each of them until I find one I can easily handle on my own and bring it in the shop and up to the man.

He already has a length of chain on the counter and looks at me with a grease smear on my face and lets out a chuckle before saying "fitty for em both."

I hand him fifty dollars in cash, thank him and lug the chain and winch out to my trunk. Looking in at the pristine trunk and then down at the greasy old winch and chain, I decide to go back in and buy a tarp from him. Luckily, he has a couple of the big blue plastic ones still in the package, in a box in the corner. So I hand him the cash and head back out to the car.

Knowing it was going to be a dirty job, I had left the wet wipes on the ground outside the driver's side door, so I cleaned my hands best I could before opening up the tarp and wrapping the winch up and placing it in the trunk. I then thoroughly clean my hands, arm and face off with nearly the entire container before getting in and heading back to the highway.

In Memphis, Tennessee, I stop for the chloroform, medical bag and surgical gloves. I find them all at a medical supply store and the clerk didn't even look twice at me. I cannot help but wonder what else they might sell here and to whom. After hitting the store and stashing the last of the supplies in the wheel well under the rug in the trunk, I check the GARMIN and it tells me it will be about nineteen more hours before I get home. I decide to attempt to make that last stretch in one shot and get home to Dean. It has been a little over two days since I left Modesto, over three since I last spoke to him and I just want to get home.

About three quarters of the way there, I start getting really tired and give Dean a call. He is still not answering, so I leave a message telling him I am about five hours out and really tired and could use someone to talk to so I do not fall asleep. A few minutes later the phone rings, startling me back to consciousness. I had not even realized I was falling asleep and it scared me so I pull onto the shoulder and answer.

Dean sounds frantic when I first pick up, hearing the weariness in my voice. He tells me that I need to stop and get some sleep because he would rather wait a few extra hours to see me alive than to have to drive several to see me dead. He apologizes for not picking up and explains that he needed time to think about everything but when he heard my last message, he knew he was being an idiot.

I had pulled back onto the road while he was talking and am approaching Michaux State Forest in Fayetteville, Pennsylvania, so I decide to make a final stop for sleep.

Dean asks me to give him a call when I am about an hour out so he can meet me at my apartment, but I ask him if I can call him when I get home since I have not showered in days and would really love to be clean before seeing him.

He laughs and wishes me sweet dreams before hanging up.

Too tired to set up the tent again, I just lay the seat back and I am asleep before I even let go of the handle. I sleep longer than I had planned, having forgotten to set a timer before crashing, and I rush back onto the road. It takes me a little over four hours to get home, and I enjoy pulling my car into my own parking spot for the first time. I keep the supplies locked in the trunk, planning on making a run to the church in a day or two to drop them off and I gather together everything in my passenger seat. As I am in the elevator, I give Dean a call and tell him to come over and that he can just let himself in. I dump the bag of garbage from my car into the incinerator chute and stumble into my apartment. Dropping my travel bags on the floor outside my room, I head straight for the shower. I strip my clothes off, throwing them into the corner by the door. It's been days since I have had a proper shower, washing my hair and body in bathroom sinks and with wet wipes just does not compare. As I step into the steaming hot shower, I let out a soft moan of pleasure. The hot water flowing down my skin not only washes away the dirt, but it also gets rid of all the tension of all the driving.

Eventually, I hear a hesitant knock at the bathroom door and Dean calls in to me.

With a big smile, I invite him in and together we get rid of the last of the tension. Dean and I end up going straight to sleep after the shower. He tried to get me to eat first, but I think the dark circles and pale face won out and instead, he sweeps me up and carries me into the bedroom, where we cuddle up and I quickly fall asleep in his arms.

Chapter 14

I hear the bedroom door opening and suddenly, I smell something delicious. Wiping sleep from my eyes, I see Dean standing at the side of the bed with a plate in one hand and a mug of what smells like good strong coffee in the other. I sit up and he carefully sets the plate on my lap on top of the blankets. There are scrambled eggs, French toast, sausages, and some fresh berries on the plate, and he places the coffee on my end table.

I ask Dean where the food came from and he tells me he went shopping after I called to let him know I was on my way home and he stocked the refrigerator for me, so I would have plenty of food in the house.

He was surprised I had not noticed until I explained I didn't make it past the shower before he got here. He laughs and kisses me on the forehead and then lets me know he would be right back, before jogging out of the room.

When he returns with his own plate and glass of orange juice, he catches me with a big mouthful. I try to smile and must look really goofy because he chuckles and carefully sits down next to me on the bed.

He asks how the drive was, and I tell him about the incident at the rest stop and how for the most part it was uneventful.

I go on about the scenery as well, and then I thank him for lending me the supplies.

After telling me he was glad I made it home okay, he got this sad look on his face but before he could say anything, I sigh and say "Give me a couple weeks and we can start looking for an apartment together."

He is stunned, sitting there with his left hand holding his plate, his right gripping the fork that rests on the edge of the plate, a look of puzzlement on his face. I had been thinking about it the entire trip and I knew I would lose Dean if I did not make a commitment of some kind as soon as I got home. I also knew I planned to have my situation with the evil man out of the way within a week and a half. I want to watch him for a week and then I will take him down and do what needs to be done. Two weeks to start looking, it would be at least another week before we found something. This should work.

When he finally gets his wits together and the magnitude of my statement finally settles in, Dean grabs my plate and sets both our plates on the floor. Before I have a chance to protest, he has me back against the bed and he is smothering me with soft loving kisses. I guess he accepts my deal. After he has gotten that out of his system, he hands me my food back and with a final kiss on my neck, he lets me finish the meal in a content silence.

Dean and I then spend the entire day together, most of it in the bedroom. When we finally venture out, he asks to see the car.

I tell him he can see everything but in the trunk because I've not cleaned my mess out of there yet and it is a disaster from my trip.

With a laugh he tells me he understands and will not ask to see in there. He then jokes that he's not as much a trunk man as what's under the hood, and then he winks at me.

Hand in hand, we walk outside and I show off my new baby. One of the things I made sure to do was hit a drive-through car wash every now and then to get the road dirt off her. Dean is impressed and makes several approving noises and head nods when checking over the engine.

When he is finished, he asks if he can take her for a test drive.

Nervously, I say okay and get in the passenger seat, handing him the keys. It is a short trip around the neighborhood but enough for him to grin and tell me he now understands why I had to do it. As we are stopped at a red light, I reach over and give him a big kiss, then we return to the parking lot.

He asks to spend the night again since he will be working a ten hour shift tomorrow, and would not be getting out until after I go in to work.

With a big smile I ask "Pizza or Chinese?" as we head back up to my apartment.

Just for one day, I tell myself, I will have a normal life. As we ride up the elevator, I snuggle into him, breathing in his scent, knowing all is perfect. I just hope it stays perfect.

Dean leaves early the next morning and with working a long shift, it gives me the perfect opportunity to head out to the church and drop off all the supplies I purchased. On my way out, I stop at one of the bait and tackle shops and pick up the last few supplies I will need; including duct tape, fish hooks, fuels, rags and a box of matches. Finally I make a stop and a little mom-and-pop store for some lemon juice, scouring pads, a bottle of rubbing alcohol, a package of cleaning gloves and a two pack of Exacto blades.

The elderly lady behind the counter comments on how she is glad she does not have to scrub anything anymore and smiles as she hands me my change.

I drive the rest of the way lost in thoughts about Dean and what is to come. I wonder if he will still love me after I complete my task. Will I even be the same person? I try to imagine how this will change me as a whole and then decide there is no point dwelling over what is to come. As I drive up to the old chain, I am very careful, slowly creeping in so as not to disturb the road too much. I do not want it to be visibly obvious someone has been here. I've backed in so that my trunk is right up against the chain without actually touching it.

After the car is parked, I head out to the church to check things out, and it takes several trips to unload everything. I stash the things in a deep closet I found in what was once the office and I lock the door with the new lock I installed on my last trip out. I had put the gloves on before moving everything, and I made sure to wipe everything I could down with the rubbing alcohol so as to hopefully remove any prints in case my stash happens to be found before I can use them. Looking over the items, I now have everything I need except for the evil man, but that will be remedied soon enough. Going back to my car, I wipe down the trunk and put all the rags and supplies in a garbage bag.

On my way home, I hit one of those self-serve car wash places. First I hit the interior cleaning area. I clean out any last bits of garbage that I find in the cabin area and tuck the wet wipes in the glove box before using their industrial vacuum to clean it and the trunk out. I use their vending machine to get some interior vinyl and upholstery wipes as well as some of glass wipes.

After thoroughly cleaning out the interior, I finish by using some of the protectant spray and a rag that was left in the trunk with another faded sticky note saying 'Always wipe my baby down inside with this, after cleaning."

With the interior done, I moved to the trunk, where I gave it equal care. I check the trunk for any stains and spray it with some car upholstery freshener spray. From there, I pull into one of the wash bays, where I clean her off both top and bottom. Pulling out into the space behind the building, I use an old towel to dry her off before rubbing on the wax. When I am satisfied she looks as good as when I first picked her up, I head home and get ready for work.

Over the next few days, I plan and prepare and now I am ready. It is the first night of my five day stake-out and excitedly, I stand in the shadows behind the dumpster, dressed in the outfit I tested with my previous rehabilitation job. Dean had to go away this morning for a week-long training session, so this is the perfect time to do this. I will not have to worry about finding excuses to not go on a date or have to explain why I am so tired after having a night home alone to sleep in, or not answering my phone when he knows I should be home. My feelings for Dean could have gotten in the way otherwise, but now I do not have to worry about that; I can do what needs to be done and move on. I can watch that monster, find out when and where to strike and complete my task before Dean even returns, and hopefully have a day to recover. I made an appointment at a day spa for the day before he is expected home. I am hoping that it will cleanse away any last residue of that evil man and leave me physically renewed, since my soul will finally have its cleansing after I am done. I will finally be able to start that new life with the man of my dreams, and my nightmares will be put to rest.

Sitting on the sidewalk across from the store, I am waiting for the evil man to leave his job. My plan is to follow him each night and learn his routines. I am dressed like a vagabond and sit with my head lowered and a stained, Styrofoam coffee cup sitting beside me with a couple quarters in it. Nobody notices the homeless; that was his trick and now I will use it as well. Although I could not find his home, my research paid off as I managed to figure out where he works. I watch the shop go dark and then he comes out of the building alone, a rolled up paper tucked under his left arm. He scans the street both ways and then pulls down the gate, setting the padlocks in place on either side. He looks down the street to the right of the shop again before he turns left and starts walking toward the corner, completely oblivious to the homeless woman across the street. Such arrogance, he did not even take a second to look me over, as if I were some piece of trash discarded and left to blow away in the wind.

As he gets halfway down the block, I make a note in my little notepad. I had picked up a new one just for this task; an Ed Hardy's *Love Kills Slowly* graphic dons the front of it. Reconnaissance is the most important thing for me right now; I have to be sure nothing goes wrong. Know everything, see everything, and expect everything, which is what will keep me from messing up. As I follow him, I wonder if he did this with me or if I just happened to be in the wrong place at the wrong time. I wonder if I should ask him that when I have him alone, then I decide not to ask, as it could be read as a form of weakness. He stops at the corner and waits for the light to change, even though there is no traffic on the road. My clothes are dark and dirt covered, as is my face, so I easily blend into the shadows between buildings, where I can watch him unseen when he stops.

Crossing the street, he goes about halfway down the block and turns into the all night pharmacy with its bright neon lights. I wait in a dark doorway of an apartment building across the street sitting on the stoop, my legs pulled up against my body, as if chilled. Looking in through the big glass window, I watch him grab some items off the shelves, pay at the back and then he emerges and turns left to continue to the end of the block. I make notes of the name of the pharmacy, time spent inside and the items he picked up including the large box of Magnum Condoms. The man must have an exceptionally large ego to buy such a thing.

When he reaches the end of the block and turns left, I quickly move to the corner. When I am sure it is safe, I shift diagonally across the intersection and watch him walk the last three blocks keeping a one block distance between us, always from a doorway or alley. I make a separate note to get different footwear, as my black boots make too much noise when I am walking quickly.

As he walks up the stairs to what I am assume is his two-story town house, he scans the street again and I wonder if he senses me or is just normally this cautious. Since my attack, I have found myself more aware but have yet to become as paranoid as he appears to be. He fishes a key ring out of the left pocket of his jacket and I watch as he selects the key with the blue ring around it and uses it to unlock the door. He walks in, and I watch until I see a light turn on just inside the door. He moves through the house as the window to the left lights up and then the one just beyond that. I write down his address and make a note to look up the records for the houses in this area, hopefully I can find a plan for his house or at least one similar so that I know which rooms he spends the most time in. Perhaps there is a pattern, something I can work from, to decide when and where to strike. Right now he is in the kitchen. I can tell this because he has sheer white curtains in the windows and I can see the cabinetry and part of his refrigerator through them. He eventually moves to the middle room again and then upstairs. By the end of the evening, I have made note of every light that was turned on and the length of time between each, until all the lights go out. I sketch up the front of the house and note which windows lit up together to help with finding the right plans. I also note which lights are turned off last, as most likely that will be his bedroom. I then wait several hours to see if he gets up again but he does not, so I head home. Once I get to the apartment, I put my things away, take a shower and go to bed. Sleep does not come easily however, as I lay there thinking about everything I saw tonight and what it all means.

For the next three days, I follow the same routine. I wake up and hit the gym for some boxing and weights, and then I return home, shower, paint and then research. Each evening, I go out to the place where he works and follow him and he goes straight home, but on the fourth night he does something different. After locking the gate, he turns right and walks three blocks, before turning left and going into a bar.

The first couple nights I dressed as a vagrant, but then I decided to try out some of the new clothes. Tonight, I am wearing the new wig and heavy make-up, as well as a bra that gives my two cup sizes and a very flattering outfit consisting of a pair of skin-tight faded black jeans and a low-cut tight mohair sweater. A silver cross on a chain dangles down between my upheaved breasts and I hope it is enough to disguise my appearance, because I need to follow him in.

Before entering the bar, I carefully peer through the window and notice him sitting at a table next to a young lady. Sitting around the bar are people ranging from business men to bikers and I know that I will not look out of place walking in here. Heading in, I walk to the end of the bar closest to where he and the woman are sitting and call for a Captain Morgan and Coke like someone who was a regular at this establishment.

The bartender soon brings me a glass and says "That's three buck, pretty lady."

I place a five dollar bill on the counter to cover the drink and a nice tip as I plan to return and talk with the bartender later and he takes it with a wolfish grin.

Working in this field, I know that if you treat the staff well from the start, you have more of a chance of finding out what you want later and by the look on his face, he's interested in more than talking with me. I take a sip of my drink and gaze casually in the mirror, pretending to fix my make-up around my eyes and checking out the other patrons, but in reality, I am watching them. He is leaning back toward the girl near him but not turning to talk with her yet. She sits there with her drink watching the door eagerly and I wonder if she waiting for a date to show up.

After about ten minutes, the girl lets out a heavy sigh and begins to stand when he stops her and offers to buy her a drink. She smiles, takes one last look at the door and joins him. The two sit for a while drinking, talking and laughing and then they get up together. I watch, hiding my disgust as they head out the door and back to his place, arm and arm. She has obviously had a bit too much to drink, as she is swaying and leaning heavily into him. I want to stop them, scream that he is evil, but I do not. My desire for revenge keeps my lips tightly closed and I hope for the best. Perhaps he will not kill her, or maybe she is his next victim and I can both save her and grab him.

As they go inside together, I see the lights go on straight up toward the bedroom. I wait in the dark, listening for a scream, watching for signs of trouble but it is silent save for the normal street noises.

After about an hour, the front door flies open and the girl leaves in a huff yelling "Thanks for nothing" over her shoulder. She stomps down the street and I follow her back to her car, writing down the license plate number, make and model.

I then hurry back to his place and notice that the downstairs light between the front entry and the kitchen is on. He then follows his normal routine through and when his lights all go off, I head back to the bar.

I sit back on the end of the bar where I was before and the bartender comes over and asks if I want another drink.

I nod and put another five on the bar after he sets my drink down on a coaster decorated with several ring stains.

Curious, he asks why I left so suddenly with half a drink in my glass only to return and buy another, and I tell him I was seeing what my "boyfriend" was up to when he was supposedly sick.

The bartender laughs and then apologizes to me with a "If he's your man, then you better just dump him because he's in here every week and leaves with some new young thing. Funny thing is, the girl he hooks up with is always here for a date she arranged on some dating site and they are always stood up."

I thank him for his advice and the information and he gives me his number on a napkin.

I finish my drink off and head to an all-night café down the street that offers free internet and computer service with a purchase. After ordering a double cappuccino with a shot of peppermint and a swish of chocolate, I sit down at one of the many open computers. Using Officer Pacitti's password that I watched him type in during one of my many visits to see if they found any more information, I log into the DMV's website and find an address to go with the car. I write it down and plan my visit.

Going home, I quickly change my outfit, putting on a different wig and makeup. I then head over to the apartment of Miss Annabelle Wilkins, who lives in the village.

Banging on the door like a pissed off girlfriend, I have prepared myself to play the role on my way over.

When Annabelle opens, it I spout out obscenities, as well as accusing her of being a whore.

She backs up slightly, trying to close the door but I push my way in and when she is finally able to get a word in, frantically she asks what this is about.

I spit "You fucked my boyfriend tonight, you whore. I watched you leaving his place and followed you home! I've been standing out there, trying to calm down enough to not rip your hair right out of your head."

She holds her hands up defensively and sputters about how she didn't know and how sorry she is. She then tells me that he treated her horribly in the bedroom and didn't even care she wasn't enjoying herself. She tells me that he was verbally abusive too, and that I am better off getting away from him as soon as possible.

I allow an expression of sorrow and defeat cross my face before I tell her I am expecting his child and that I am stuck with him.

Deep sorrow crosses her face before she asks me to stay for a bit to talk. My planned worked; she feels sorry for me and will tell me whatever she knows about him now.

She motions me toward the couch. "Would you like some tea?" she asks and I shake my head no, so she joins me on the couch.

I sit down with my head lowered and my hands clasped in my lap. Sitting down next to me, she takes my hands and asks why I cannot just leave him anyway.

Having been at the sessions at the Y I knew just what to say, how to play the victim. I let out a sob and tell her a story of how he has me convinced I am nothing without him and that nobody else would ever love me because I am worthless and since I am carrying his kid, it makes me tainted goods. "Who would want to be with a woman, raising someone else's child?"

This pisses her off and she tells me how he has been lying to me and that I needed to get away from him; if he treats me this way, imagine how he will treat the child.

I go on to say I wish I could but he has keys to my apartment and a special trinket my grandmother gave me on her deathbed stashed in a drawer in his bedroom and that he refuses to give me a key or the code to his place and will not give them back. It's how he controls me; he says that he will destroy the necklace and then wait for me in my apartment and beat me until I lose the baby.

Annabelle vents her frustration and then gets a pleased look on her face. With a mischievous grin she grabs a notepad and pen off the coffee table,

"Here's the code I watched him punch in the alarm box when we went in the place" she says as she hands me the slip of paper. "If you can get inside, this will at least let you shut off the alarm."

I ask how she knew it and she told me she watched a movie once where this guy set an alarm to keep a woman locked in a prison cell and the woman got out because she watched him punch in the numbers one time. It made a lot of sense, oddly enough, and I got a new sense of respect for this woman. She may not be all that smart about picking up men, but at least she knows how to take care of herself, just in case.

She also tells me he tried to get her to join him at his cabin upstate, as he supposedly goes there every weekend and wanted her to come along this weekend. He had shown her pictures and a brochure about it in his bedroom before they got into bed. She goes on to say how she was really freaked out about this because he was so detached during sex and was only focused on his own pleasure, yet he wants to take her upstate for a private weekend. Something seemed really fishy about that, and now that she met me, she says it all makes sense.

"He wanted to get more action without getting caught! He was obviously trying to turn me into his second lover or something."

I knew that wasn't the case however, it appears he is trying a new tactic at acquiring his victims. Now I know I am running out of time, since he is obviously trying to find new prey.

I ask if he mentioned where the cabin is and she tells me that he said something about five miles north of this small town and told me where he tucked the brochure after he showed it to her.

I thank her for everything and give her a hug before I leave and promise to never go back to that "bastard" again.

Annabelle hugs me back and wishes me luck. I head out the door with just what I need to complete my plans.

From Annabelle's, I go back home and prepare for the next day. While the evil man is at work, I will find a way into his house and search for the address for the cabin, as well as any other information I might need to catch him. If he goes there every weekend it will be the perfect place for me to take him down. I am barely able to sleep after I get into bed; all I can do is think about how close I am to finally completing my task. I find myself worrying about all the things that can go wrong at the house and trouble shooting them. I consider the possibility of him returning, how I might get into his home, how to handle it if the code does not work. It takes several hours for me to finally drift off into my dreams, and even there, I cannot escape my worries. I dream of being caught and the police locking me in a tiny cement cell with no lights. The rest of the night, I fight with nightmares as I toss and turn.

Chapter 15

Excitement and anticipation fill me as I watch him leave his home the next morning. I dress in a pair of tight-fitting black stretch jeans, a deep grey and black striped tee shirt and my hooded jacket. My hair is pulled back into a tight bun and I have it wrapped in a bandana and tucked under a ball cap. I am watching from behind the bushes of an apartment building across from his house, the space between the bushes and building just enough for me to slip into, and I am completely hidden unless you are intentionally looking for me.

As he steps out the front door, he looks around before turning to lock the multiple locks and clipping the keys to his waistband. After turning the last lock, he turns back to the street and scans it again before walking down the stairs to the sidewalk. I wait patiently as he moves out of view, looking down at my watch.

He has thirty minutes before his shift starts, so I watch and wait. I will occasionally bring my watch up so that I can check the time without taking my attention off his home. It would be a terrible mistake if I happen to glance down just as he returns, or someone else shows up.

Finally, it is time for his shift to start and I know the chances of him returning are slim, so I put on my medical gloves and then my black gloves over them. Tucking my hands into my pockets to hide the gloves, I head across the street and slip through the front gate. After a cursory glance around the front yard for one of those false rocks, which I do not find, I move around to the back.

As I wander around, I examine plants, leaves and roots while seeking a key so that I can say I am a gardener if anyone wanders across me and has questions. Reaching the back, I am relieved to see that he has a high fence around his yard; it will make it easier to find a way in and less chance of being seen by a nosey neighbor. After a quick search and still no luck, I scan the windows of the houses around his. I had watched cars leave the houses on both sides of his and after checking out the houses, I am pretty safe to assume they are now empty. The house directly behind his appears to have sustained fire damage, and the houses on either side were affected by it as well, so it looks like they are all currently empty.

Secure that nobody will see me, I start trying to open the windows along the back of his house that I can reach. All of the windows are closed and it appears the lower ones are all locked and his basement windows are those solid glass blocks. I am starting to worry, when I notice not all of them are blocks.

To the left, tucked behind a rose bush, is a window covered with a board and a vent sticking out of it. Checking to be sure all my hair is tucked away tightly, I slink over and carefully prop the rose bush out with a shovel I found earlier in the garden. I check the board and it is loose. The wood had started rotting around the screws and it easily popped off with almost no sound.

Carefully, I set it aside and look into the basement. Directly below the window is a washer and dryer, and across the room I notice a small box near the ceiling with a flashing red light on it. It must be a sensor for his alarm system which means as soon as I get within range I will have ninety seconds to get upstairs and turn the alarm off. I take note of the direction the basement stairs lead and peek through the windows closest to where it should end. When I reach the back door and look in, I see a partially open door down the hall. Heading back to the basement I see the door is slightly ajar, so there is a pretty good chance it is the same door. I head back to the back door and look for a keypad, hoping he had one installed at both doors so that I will not have to navigate my way blindly through his apartment and find the one near the front. I begin to worry, until I notice what may be the keypad peeking out behind a jacket hung on a hook just inside the door. I say a silent prayer to any god that might hear it that it is the keypad.

Quickly, I head back to the open basement window and look in again and then take another look around to be sure nobody is watching me. I pull a garbage bag from my jacket pocket, opening it up and spreading it out on the ground in front of the window. Carefully I sit on the bag and remove my shoes, placing them on the ground under the rose bush and turn toward the open window, planning my moves. Quickly, I slip through the window and fold the bag over, placing it on top of my sneakers.

Slipping off the dryer, the alarm starts making its detected motion sound and I hustle up the stairs. Moving the jacket I let out a sigh of relief as I punch in the code Annabelle gave me. Thankfully it works and the green light flips on just as the beeping stops. I head back down to the basement and check to be sure nobody saw me entering the house and look to be sure I didn't disturb anything on my way in.

When I am sure everything is clean and in its place, I head up the stairs and to where Annabelle mentioned I might find the address. Carefully, I make my way down the hall and up the stairs to his bedroom. Slowly, I open the drawer in the end table and there was a small piece of paper with an address for a place upstate, tucked in a pamphlet for a small community. Quickly, I write down the address in my notebook and tuck it back into my back pocket before placing everything back where I found it. I look around the place once more before heading back to the basement. Laying my plastic back out and cleaning up the small amount of dirt I knocked in on the window ledge,

I head back upstairs and reset the alarm. I leave the basement door slightly ajar and I slip out the window and out of the reach of the sensor. Peeking in, I double check to be sure I didn't drop any more dirt inside and then put my sneakers back on. I return the board to its place, careful not to splinter the wood out as I push it back over the screws. I fold up my bag and put it back in my pocket and move the shovel from the bush. Carefully, I rearranged the branches so they did not look disturbed and then I return the shovel to the garden, gently pressing the dirt back around the base where it was thrust into the ground. When everything is back in place, I take a final glance over the scene before sneaking back around the house and out the front gate, latching it just as he had, before heading home. I did it; I infiltrated his home and got the information I need, undetected.

On my way home, I stop by the library and log-in using the information I saved from a previous trip to the library. I hop on the internet search engine and look for a mapping site. It brings me to a site called Mapquest, where I type in the address for the cabin and it gives me a detailed view of where it is. I select the option to get directions to that address and use the evil man as the starting point and print up the directions and maps it gave me.

Logging out, I grab the printouts, folding and tucking them into my book and head to a gas station just down the street. There, I pick up a folding map of New York State and head home. It is Friday, and there was a good chance he will be heading out to the cabin after his shift is over tonight. If I were patient, I would wait, watch him this weekend and hold off until the following weekend to take him down, but I am not patient. I cannot allow him the chance to take one more innocent woman.

I gather everything from my hidden storage area in my bathroom and place them in a couple of garbage bags and load them into my car, telling Tommy it is some of my old clothes I am donating to the Salvation Army.

It is not the first time I did this, so he thinks nothing of it. With everything in the car I go back up to my apartment and make sure I did not leave anything behind, even the smallest scrap of paper could be my downfall.

I sit down on the couch and give Dean a call. This might be the last time I ever talk to him if things go poorly, and I want him to know how I truly feel about him.

When he picks up, he sounds worried since I never call midday without a reason.

For the first time, fear slips into me as I tell Dean that I love him and want to move forward but that I really need the weekend to truly come to terms with what it all means.

He sounds upset but tells me that he understands and will be waiting.

With a final goodbye, I hang up and cry for the first time since that horrible day. I cry because I was introduced to love and now I am putting it all on the line for revenge, but I cannot turn back. The darkness that has twined itself around my soul will not allow me true happiness until I cut it away and free myself once and for all. With a final hard sob, I take a deep breath and resolve myself to what needs to be done and after splashing my face with some cold water, I prepare to go. Grabbing my book stuffed with printouts and other loose papers, I head to the door. Before closing the door, I take one last look at my apartment; at my paintings lining the hallway and of the painting of the dove I put at the end last night; and I say goodbye to that part of me. As I close and lock the door, I silently say a goodbye, just in case.

Normally I play music of some kind when I am driving, but today I drive in silence, my thoughts too loud to hear anything else over. My cell phone is turned off, battery removed and placed in a baggie with my wallet in the glove compartment. I look over at it occasionally, wondering if I should have just left them and all other forms of identification home, but decide I did the right thing bringing them, just in case.

As I am exiting the city, I look at my watch and note that I have at least four more hours before the man even gets out of work. Plenty of time for me to find the place, hide my car, scope it out and make my plans. With the directions on my passenger seat, I drive three more hours to the cabin. I find the mailbox at the end of a well-worn stone road. Carefully I drive down the road and let out a breath when I find there are no cars here, which hopefully means the place is empty. I turn the car around so it's facing down the driveway and park. Getting out, I look around; it is so quiet and peaceful. Completely surrounded by woods, it is set back at least a mile or so from the road. I look up at the small cabin, which fits the stereotype perfectly. Built with wood logs bigger around than my head, a faded wooden deck wraps around it and there are old wooden shutters on all the windows. I wonder if I am at the right place as I walk up the stairs to the front door. Peeking in, I see the interior is decorated exactly as his home is, good chance it belongs to him.

I get back in my car and drive down the long driveway, turning the opposite direction on the road from which I came. I had not noticed any good places to park my car on the way here, so I hoped there would be something a little further down the road. Sure enough, about a quarter of a mile down I find a 'scenic pull-off' and pull in.

Parking the car, I take the directions to the cabin and head over to one of the grills they placed for tourists next to a picnic bench and placed them in it. With a small squirt of lighter fluid and a flick of a match the evidence is destroyed in a flash. I do not need directions from here to my church because once I back tracked back to the highway, I know the way and it was only about another hour to an hour and a half to get there from here. Perfect.

Suddenly, I realize I still have a minimum of four hours before he would be getting here, and that is if he comes straight after work. I also realized I forgot to look in his garage to see what kind of car he drives. Cursing my mistakes, I get in the car and drive back toward the highway and pull into a little diner's parking lot. I had a lot of time to kill, so I decide to get something to eat. I put on my wig and some make-up to hide my appearance as well as put on a black hoodie and zip it up.

Walking in I see a few locals sitting at the counter chatting over some pie and coffee and the elderly woman behind the counter yells to me, "Take a seat anywhere you like, sweetie, and I will be right over."

I move to a booth in the corner with a good view of the road so I can keep an eye out without looking like I am watching it. It is not one of the main stretches and from what I have seen so far, it's hardly used, so any cars driving by would be easy to scope out. Shortly after I sit, she approaches with a coffee mug and a pot of steaming coffee.

"Can I start you off with some coffee, hun?"

Nodding I say thank you as she pours me a cup and hands me the menu. "Just give a holler when you're ready to order, sweetie. My name's Jannie."

I give her a smile and another "Thanks" as she slowly moves back to her place behind the counter and goes back to chatting with her friends.

I look down at the menu and try to decide what to get. I do not have to worry about eating light since it will have plenty of time to settle, so I decide on the bacon cheddar burger with fries.

I yell my order to Jannie to save her the walk and she thanks me before putting it in.

Quietly, I sit looking out the window, listening to the friendly chatter and smelling the food cooking. About ten minutes later, Jannie is setting a plate down in front of me with a large burger overflowing with toppings sitting next to a large pile of steak cut fries and a big dill pickle spear.

My eyes go huge and Jannie, laughs telling me I could use a few pounds and then she asks if I need anything else.

I giggle and jokingly request a roll of paper towels and a hallow leg. She walks away, snickering, and I go to work on the huge plate of food.

I am only able to finish half the burger, the entire pickle and about a third of the fries, the rest she boxes up for me and tucks in a bag with a slice of the apple pie "on the house."

I thank her, leaving a big tip and head out to my car. At least if it ends up being my last meal, it was a good one.

I drive back to the over-look and park. There's still another two or three hours before he would be getting here, so I might as well work on a plan of how to get him from here to my church. I had thought of it somewhat but there were still gaps that could not be filled, until I saw what I had to work with at the cabin. Tucked under my seat is a bottle of chloroform and a clean rag in a baggie. I plan to use that to knock him out. I sit there for hours, working over different plans in my head until I have one I think will work beautifully. I find myself munching on the pie as I work over my ideas. It is homemade and tastes amazing. As I take the final bite, I look at my watch and realize it's nearly an hour past the earliest time he would have been arriving. I have been sitting here eating by moonlight and completely lost track of the time.

I reach under the seat and pull out the baggie, and step outside. I head over to a tree, and removing the bottle, I pour some onto the rag inside the bag, carefully holding my breath until the bottle is closed and the baggie is sealed back up. I tuck the bottle back under my seat and place the baggie on my passenger seat. I take a gallon of water and make up some mud in the dirt by the lot in front of my car which I then coat my plates with it, as well as both my bumpers, making it look like I've been doing a little off-roading. I also make sure to splatter mud along the sides behind the tires. I then pull out the map, unfolding it, crinkling it some and spread it over the bag on the passenger seat facing me. I rub my eyes a little smearing the make-up and making me look very tired before getting back on the road and heading back to the cabin. I see a car turning onto the drive as I come around the corner and excitement courses through me. Could it be him? I pull over and wait about five minutes before continuing down his driveway. In my hand, I hold a sticky note with a poorly written address that could easily be mistaken for his or a couple of the others on this section of road.

As I pull up I see the lights are on inside and he is coming out the door. I come to a stop not far from where I parked earlier and shut off my headlights to "be polite" as he comes around the front of the car and to my open window. With my dimmed overhead light on, he leans in, noting my weary expression and the map.

"You lost?" he asks as he leans further in the window nearly in my face.

I nod my head and point to the address on the note and he stands back up as I tell him I cannot figure out that address and I've been up and down this road and every driveway I can find looking for this "damn guy's place." I further explain that I cannot get any reception out here on my cell phone.

He offers to have me go inside with him so that I can use his wired phone to get a hold of my friend and as he walks toward the front of my car, I grab the rag out of the bag.

I quickly move up behind him and without hesitation jump on his back and with both hands holding the rag over his nose and mouth. He starts to fight but goes down quite fast, and I wonder if I put too much on it. Without a second thought I run to the trunk and grab the zip ties and another clean rag. Returning to him, I bind his wrists behind his back and bind his ankles together and then gag him, just in case. I then pull out the Creeper from my trunk. It's this really handy device that allows you to roll under your car to work on it, and it is perfect for moving his body to my passenger side. I roll him onto it and move him around. Opening the door, I prop him up and carefully move him into the seat after moving the map. I place him upright and check the bindings, as well as the gag. I then place an acupuncture needle in a spot for paralyzing him, just in case. After I have him settled, I go inside the cabin and grab his coat, as well as a pair of fishing gloves and a hat on the table below the hook his coat is on. I shut off all the lights, hide his fishing poles in a closet out of view and lock the place up with his keys from his coat pocket.

Returning to the car, I carefully place his coat around him, buttoning it up and put the seat belt in place. Situating the arms of the coat as if he were asleep with his hands in his lap, I tuck the gloves in the sleeves. I then put the hat on his head and tilt his head forward, hiding his face under the large brim and in the collar of his coat. With the seat slightly tipped back and the seat belt in place, he should be secure enough for the drive. To someone looking in, he looks like he's sound asleep after a long fishing trip. Satisfied, I carefully turn around and head to my church. There is no going back now.

Chapter 16

I have removed the acupuncture needle and when he revives, he finds himself suspended from the ceiling of an old church by his wrists, and his feet tethered to the stage beneath him. Duct tape secures his wrists together, as well as his ankles. His head is shaved clean and there is duct tape going clear around it, binding his mouth closed completely. The room is dark but for the candles lit around him in a circle on the ground. He looks over at a bag similar to his own, sitting on the podium, with a large white candle burning beside it. The church is completely silent, not even the insects make a sound, as if they too are waiting in anticipation. I have stripped him down to his briefs and I can see the cool air affecting his skin. Small bumps have erupted over his entire body, and he is shivering slightly. His head whips around as he scans the room. I imagine he is trying to figure out where he is and how he got here. I watch as he goes still and moves his head, tilting it slightly, listening. From behind him I laugh, but it is not a joyous sound, it is bitter and harsh and makes his head snap straight. Slowly, I walk around from behind him, the whoosh of fabric the only sound he hears. I am wearing a black hooded robe that goes all the way down to my feet which are clad in smooth black oriental style silk slippers. The hood covers my face, hiding it in shadows. I am careful, avoiding the candles so that there is no light on my face as I approach him. By now I am sure he can smell the incense that has clung to my robe.

Leaning in toward him I whisper, "Revenge is sweet, and it is mine."

Throwing back the hood, I laugh at the recognition and fear on his face. He knows who captured him, who chained him in the church, who is about to exact their revenge on him and he is very afraid, because he can see the hatred in my face. I can see it in his eyes. I draw my pointed metal finger nails down his cheek in a painful caress, leaving lines of blood forming in the swelling gouges. He starts flailing his head from side to side and I laugh again and ask him if he enjoys receiving as much as he does giving. His head stops and we lock eyes, at first his gaze is filled with disgust and hate, but it soon turns to fear and he tries to plead with me. I slowly bring my gaze to the bag on the podium, knowing he will follow my gaze and is now staring at the bag as well.

"I bet you are wondering what is in there, aren't you?" I ask as I slowly walk toward the bag, caressing my hand across the top of it.

He tries to flail, but his body did not budge. He stares up into the darkness but cannot see how he is secured. Seeing his attention moved from the bag to the ceiling, I decide to throw him a bone and tell him how I suspended him. I tell him

"There is a chain through a large eye bolt in the ceiling, the chain goes down to a winch behind the pews on the wall over there" as I motion off to the side with my head. "With your feet secured to the bolt below you, I was easily able to raise you up nice and taut, so you can't move."

An evil grin creeps across my face as I finish with "so much easier than drugs, and you get to suffer through every last moment of what I have in store for you."

I reach into the bag and pull out a pouch and walk over to him with a crooked grin on my face. I look into his eyes and allow him to see only hatred and vengeance, what he put there and what he will now suffer. I have felt the pain every day since he tormented me, it is like a bug that has burrowed just beneath my skin, and itching, but I am unable to scratch it. Now it is his turn to feel the pain, now he will wish for death, while I make him suffer deep within his soul.

As I continue staring him in the eyes I pull out a box of acupuncture needles and a scroll. I show him the box before setting it onto the podium with the empty pouch and then I unroll the scroll and show it to him. On the scroll is a drawing of a man, front and back views, with red points marked on it. Below the illustrations it reads *"Acupuncture points to avoid due to severe pain and nerve issues."* He looks again and sees that there are penciled numbers by each of the points. He starts flailing his head as I removes the first pin from the packet and with the scroll in hand, carefully insert it into the point marked 1. He starts convulsing in pain, his eyes wide, as I place the second pin and then the third. I step back and watch him flailing, tears streaming down his face.

"I bet you never considered using something so simple, did you?" I ask as I remove the pins in the same order I placed them dropping them into a stone bowl filled with torch oil.

His head had dropped to his chest and he is still, his breathing short and ragged. Lifting his chin up to look into his face, I see he's on the verge of unconsciousness.

"Awwww, broken already? We can't have that" I state as I place a pin near the base of his neck relieving him of some the pain.

He sighs and his body stops the slight twitching it had been doing. Waiting for him to believe it might be over, I prepare the next three pins. I remove the one that is relieving the pain and carefully place it back into its plastic sleeve on the podium to the side of the box; it is the only pin that will be reused. I then pick up the next pin and set it in place, followed by the next two. The pain seems to be affecting him worse this round and I wonder if he will pass out, as I slip the third pin into his inner thigh. His body spasms yet again and he appears to be trying to shake the pins free from his body. Each movement causes his legs to hit against each other uncontrollably. Digging the pin in his thigh deeper, his skin rips and causes more intense pain. His head falls slack and I realize that he reached his tolerance level, so I take out the pins and replace the relief one. There were still four more pins to go, so I will divide them in half after he recovers. As he slowly revives for the second time, he hears music playing; it seems to be coming from all around as the sound bounces off the perfectly acoustic walls.

Time always seems to be passing by
It never waits for me
If I could do it all one more time, I wouldn't change a thing.
I feel so hollow, I feel so hollow
I feel so hollow, I feel so hollow
Time to do what's best for me. I believe I can change.

The song is by a band called Godsmack and I thought it was perfect for this particular moment. He looks around for me but I am not in his view, although I am very close, waiting for the next song to begin, waiting for my cue. I take slow even breaths, relaxing, preparing. As "Hurt" by Nine Inch Nails starts playing, he feels the prick of the pin in his back and the searing pain that follows as I begin my work from behind him. When the second pin is placed in his shoulder blade, he screams through the tape but only a muffled sound could be heard. I rub my hand on his ribs as I walk around in front of him, just as he had with me. Standing inches from his body, I am sure he can feel the heat radiating from mine as I stare into his eyes.

"I will make you hurt" I sing with Trent and then step back from him.

At that moment, I decide to not be merciful after all and place the last two pins in simultaneously. His head flies back as his body gives a hard spasm, and then another and finally he slumps just as the song ends. I laugh, but it is not my normal laugh and nowhere near a happy one. It is not even the bitter laugh I used when I first started this evening. No, it was a new laugh, one filled with emptiness and hatred and revenge, one similar to what I heard from him that day. It is the laugh of the new me, the secret me, the one that shall strike fear into those men that think they are above the law and can hurt women without consequence.

As I emit that evil cackle, I remove the four pins and replace the relief one but only briefly. When I feel he is coherent enough, I remove the pin and place it in the bowl with the rest. He is shaking from the pain, his body near shock but not allowing him the relief. Taking the bowl full of used pins, the packaging and pouch, I head to the back of the church where a large stone platform sits. I set the bowl in the center of the platform, placing the packaging and pouch inside it and then spray some lighter fluid over the items and step back a step. I pull out a box of matches from my robe's pocket and striking the red tip against the black strip on the box. It ignites. I toss the lit match into the bowl and it explodes in a ball of fire and then slowly burns until all that is left is some ash, smoke and a bitter smell in the air.

Turning, I look at him. He has slipped into unconsciousness and the muscles in his jaw have finally stilled. Returning to his limp body, I pull out some smelling salts to wake him as well as give him a couple hard slaps.

When he comes around, he is pleading with his eyes but I feel no mercy as I head back to the bag on the podium for my next surprise.

I pull out another pouch. This one contains the fish hooks and electro-shock device I had modified. Holding it up to him, I explain

"I wanted you to experience the part you seemed to enjoy doing to me so much."

I place the device and box of hooks onto the podium and then go to retrieve the now empty bowl with a towel to keep from burning myself. I set it on the ground to my right, where I have easy access but where it is not in the way. Standing up, I pull the first hook from the box, the barb has been filed down so that it will easily pull back out without ripping the flesh up. I blow against his left nipple causing it to become erect, grasping it securely I give it a pull and shoves the hook through, careful to not impale myself in the process. He tries to scream through the tape again as blood trickles down his chest and I do the same to the other one. I give him a moment to calm his breathing so he does not hyperventilate and then add hooks to both his ears and the top of his belly button. My plan is to put jewelry in each of the holes so that they will not look so suspicious when I am done but for now the hooks will be so much more fun to work with.

During my time following him, I found out he has a thing against men with piercings so what better punishment than to leave him looking like those he despises most. As I walk back to the podium, I exclaim

"Oh gee, I forgot something in the pouch" and pull a spool of wire out. It is a fine and smooth wire that slips easily through the loops in the ends of the hooks.

I begin at his belly button, moving up through the left nipple, up to the left ear, back down to the left nipple, across to the right nipple, ear, nipple and then back down through the belly button where I twist the ends together and leave a tail that reaches the closest pew. I place the spool in the bowl and retrieve the device, placing it on the pew where the wire ends. Carefully, I attach the wire into the device, holding it in my lap as I sit on the back of the pew with my feet on the seat. I make sure the wire is held taut between the device and him. Looking up at him, I grin as I hit the first switch which sends short bursts of electric through the wire. I can see by his physical reaction that he is enjoying this, so I decide to turn it up a little. His enthusiasm wilts immediately as tears stream down his face. I turn off the power and laugh before turning it back on again, higher this time. I alternate between pleasure and pain until his body stops reacting to the pleasure and tears run down his cheeks.

As he hangs there, weeping, I place a pin I had left on the podium in a spot that paralyzes his body. I do not want him ruining my piercing holes by ripping any of them out as I am placing the jewelry in. Carefully I pull out each hook, following it with a gold hoop. Dangling from the hoop is a small dagger charm. Once the last hoop is in place, I pull out the pin and walk behind him. He flails his head from side to side in fear of what is next, when I return carrying a large mirror. I hold it up for him to see my handy work and I can see he is appalled by the furrowed brow and dark eyes. When he starts shaking furiously, I flick one of the nipple daggers and he stops suddenly and glares at me, bringing forth that hard cold laugh from my lips. I take the mirror back to where I retrieved it and return with a bottle of torch oil on my left hand. Fear grips him as I stand before him holding up the bottle. I leave him wondering if I am going to set him alight for a few more moments. Then I pick up the bowl and head to the back of the church. I had placed all the items from my last trial in the bowl and now I place it back on the marble slab, dousing the contents with oil and ensuring there is a decent pool in the base to continue the burning. I then step back and see the bowl ablaze. Content with the flames I take the bottle of oil back behind him and he watches the bowl and its contents blazing.

I return to see him staring fixedly on the flames and I whisper into his ear "The marble of the bowl contains the flame but will not melt under the high heat of the special oil. That stuff will even melt metal… wonderful stuff for getting rid of evidence… …of all kinds."

He hears a timer go off and I look behind him.

"Oh no… looks like our time together is running short. Guess I need to get to the grand finale."

Walking over to the bag for the last time, I pull out one of those lemon shaped bottles of juice, a metal scouring pad and an Exacto knife. I set each tool onto the podium and then turn to him,

"Do you remember what you did to me right before you used me for a punching bag? Can you imagine the pain the citric acid causes in the cuts? I'm sure you can, otherwise why would you have done it to me. Right?"

He frantically flails his head back and forth as I raise the scrubbing pad to his chest, "No? Not your chest? Perhaps lower?"

Without waiting for a response, I vigorously rub the pad on his stomach, abrading the skin just below his belly button and then to either side and above it. I take out my anger on him, pressing the coarse pad into his tender flesh. I then pop the lid on the bottle and squirt the juice onto the raw skin in quick small bursts, watching him jump with each drop. Once again, he flails his body like a fish out of water and I cackle, knowing he will never forget this as I never forgot what he had done to me. I walk around him, pad in right hand and bottle in left and do the same to the spot between his shoulder blades and then on his lower back.

Once I am done there, I return to his view and kneel down in front of him. He is terrified of where I might decide to work next, but the pain was already near excruciating and so he hoped he would pass out from it. When I reach for between his legs, he holds his breath and vibrates in fear until I go for his inner thighs, scraping and squirting, making sure to get the spot he ripped open with the needle earlier, masking the initial damage. When the bottle is near empty, I take the razor and carve "EVIL" into his chest and squirt the last of the juice into it. His body shakes, tears streaming down his face as he finally passes out. I allow him this small bit of relief, as it aids in my plans.

Satisfied, I unhook his feet from the hook beneath him and walk to the wall where I crank him eighteen yards into the air and secure him dangling there. I take a moment to look up at him, finding it ironic that he is hanging there among the descending angels. Perhaps they will seek their vengeance upon him as well. I take a moment longer to set the mirror angled so that someone entering the church from the broken wall would see him in the reflection and find him.

I then gather the last few supplies I used and place it all in a large stone cauldron on the slab where the smaller bowl sat. I douse everything with the oil and then drop the empty bottles into it, lighting it aflame, following it with the box of matches, causing a burst of fire. I take a can of red spray paint and heads to the front of the church, and in large letters, sprays "EVIL" on it as well as the sign.

I head to the road and do the same to the end of the driveway between the chain and the road. Returning to the fire, I remove my robe, exposing my nude body and hair wrapped in a plastic cap. I toss the robe and the can into the fire, along with my surgical gloves, causing another burst of flame.

Now, wearing nothing but the slippers and cap I leave through the crumbled wall and head through the woods on the path with a smile on my face. Stopping in the old cemetery, I look back at the smoke billowing from the old church and sigh. It is all over and the nightmares should end now.

Shouldn't they?

3152854R00084

Printed in Great Britain
by Amazon.co.uk, Ltd.,
Marston Gate.